Books you will enjoy
from Keyhole Crime:

THE ROLLING HEADS by Aaron Marc Stein
THE MENACE WITHIN by Ursula Curtiss
DEATH ON A BROOMSTICK
by G. M. Wilson
MURDER AS USUAL by Hugh Pentecost
ASK FOR ME TOMORROW
by Margaret Millar
RANDOM KILLER by Hugh Pentecost
WYCLIFFE AND THE SCAPEGOAT
by W. J. Burley
WELCOME TO THE GRAVE
by Mary McMullen
LETTER OF INTENT by Ursula Curtiss
THE BURGLAR IN THE CLOSET
by Lawrence Block
THE BLOOD ON MY SLEEVE
by Ivon Baker
RANSOM TOWN by Peter Alding
THE DEAD SIDE OF THE MIKE
by Simon Brett
CATCH-AS-CATCH-CAN
by Charlotte Armstrong
DOWN AMONG THE DEAD MEN
by Evelyn Harris

WYCLIFFE AND THE PEA-GREEN BOAT

W. J. Burley

KEYHOLE CRIME
London · Sydney

First published in Great Britain 1975 by
Victor Gollancz Limited

Copyright © W. J. Burley 1975

Australian copyright 1981

This edition published 1981 by
Keyhole Crime, 15-16 Brook's Mews,
London W1A 1DR

ISBN 0 263 73659 8

Made and printed in Great Britain by
Cox & Wyman Ltd., Reading

PART ONE

1953

Chapter One

ON THE MORNING of Wednesday 24th June, Morley Tremain lay, between sleeping and waking, vaguely aware of familiar sounds from the shop below and from the street. Every now and then came the jangling of the shop door-bell, a sound which had been part of the background of his life for as long as he could remember. And there were voices, his mother's and the customers', audible only as a confused murmur. Down the street, the baker, who had a hole in the roof of his mouth, was loading wire trays of cakes and bread into his van and greeting passers-by in his garbled speech.

Morley opened his eyes and looked at the clock. Half-past eight. He was on holiday, in the second week of his annual leave from his job at the clay works. He was a wages clerk, though his mother told people that he was an accountant. The sun was shining as it had been for four or five days and, through the window with its little square panes, he could see blue sky above the roofs of the houses opposite.

The shop was always busy at this time of day with people calling for their morning newspapers. The papers arrived in a large parcel, by bus, at eight o'clock and, most mornings of the year, Morley caught that same bus to work.

Alice Weekes, in her blue, linen overall, would be in the room behind the shop marking off the contents of the parcel, scribbling people's names on papers and magazines which had been ordered and ticking them off in an account book. From time to time his mother would call, in her strident shop-voice, 'Mr Taylor's *Mail*, Alice!' or, '*Guardian* for Miss Clarke!'

He closed his eyes again and thought about Alice.

She had been employed in the shop for no more than a week

when he had plucked up courage and asked her to go to the pictures with him. She had looked up, her blue eyes solemn, her lips unsmiling, 'Do you really want me to?'

He had had little experience with girls and he felt awkward and gauche in their company. The girls at the office laughed at him more or less openly. But Alice was different; her serious manner impressed him. She said little, rarely expressing a point of view about anything, but she was a good listener. When he was with her he took the lead and she seemed to expect it. In this, as in so many things, she was the very opposite of his cousin, Eunice, the only other girl with whom he had spent much time. But sometimes he wondered what might be hidden by her smooth brow, her calm eyes and her gentle, rather sad expression. Did she really hang on his every word? At any rate he had decided that she was the girl he would marry. He was twenty-two and earning good money by village standards. They had been going together for three months. But there was no hurry; step by step was his policy in everything and it usually worked. He would give his mother time to get used to the idea.

He got out of bed. A tall, skinny young man in pyjama trousers. He had prominent ribs and bony protuberances on the shoulders; jet-black hair and a pallid complexion. His chest and fore-arms were covered with fine, black hairs. He put on his glasses which enlarged and darkened his brown eyes. After a wash and shave in the little, windowless bathroom at the top of the stairs he dressed carefully. Grey slacks, white shirt, navy-blue blazer with brass buttons and a maroon tie.

Downstairs, in the living-room, one end of the dining-table had been laid for his breakfast, bread and butter already cut. All he had to do was to boil himself an egg and make tea. It was the same every morning, whether he was going to work or not and it had been the same when he was a boy and had to catch the same bus to the grammar school. In fact, nothing had really changed since his father's death when he was ten years old.

'I've never let the shop interfere with bringing up my son and it hasn't been easy, a woman on her own.'

How often had he heard his mother say that to customers?

He settled down to breakfast, a book beside his plate. His mother bustled in, as she always did, to see how he was getting on. Her greying hair was wispy and her cheeks were slightly flushed.

'All right, Morley? Got everything you want? More tea? More bread-and-butter?'

'Yes, yes. No, thank you, mother.' Ritual responses to ritual questions. He did not look up from his book.

The shop was part of a corner house in the main street of the village and the living-room window looked out on a short, narrow access-road to the harbour. When one of the fish lorries went by it blocked the light completely and its sideboard almost brushed the wall of the house.

There were tourists about, though in 1953 they were not the sole reason for the continuing existence of the village. But already, at just after nine in the morning, they were wandering down to the harbour, peering at everything, even into the room where Morley was eating his breakfast.

When he had finished he put his dishes in the sink and went through to the shop. Alice had finished marking off the papers and was serving a young man, a stranger, with cigarettes. He was smiling at something she had said and Morley turned quickly to his mother.

'I'm going out.'

'Anywhere special?'

'Just for a walk.'

He went out into the street, closing the shop door behind him. The door still had a brass handle with a thumb latch and the inscription, FRY'S C OCOLATE in white enamelled letters stuck to the glass. The H was already missing when he first noticed such things. The sign-board over the shop still carried his father's name in faded letters: SIDNEY TREMAIN. TOBACCONIST AND NEWSAGENT. They were still known as the Sidney Tremains to distinguish them from the Harry Tremains, his uncle's family.

He walked the hundred yards or so to the harbour, shoulders

back, head held high. He was always conscious of people watching him and he guessed that they made disparaging remarks as he went by in his blue blazer with the brass buttons. More like a tourist. But he told himself that he didn't care, it meant that he had got somewhere and, if he was embarrassed when his mother told people that he was an accountant, he was not unwilling to be regarded as an up-and-coming young man.

Another glorious day with the sea sparkling under a cloudless sky. The village was celebrating its Coronation Carnival Week, everything was Coronation that year. Strings of flags, bleached but gay, fluttered in the breeze and there were tubs of flowers outside some of the buildings on the waterfront.

It was half-tide and falling; there were few craft in the basin, a couple of launches running trips for visitors and a few moored dinghies. It was the long-lining season and the fishing boats were at sea, not due back until evening. Tourists had taken over the fishermen's quay-side seats, long baulks of timber propped up on concrete blocks.

He went for a walk on the cliffs and came back for lunch which, because of the shop, was a cold dish with meat out of a tin. After lunch he was in the shop with Alice; his mother was lying down as she always did at this time. It was a quiet time of day with few customers and Alice was unpacking cartons of cigarettes and stacking them on the shelves. For a long time he was content to watch her at work, scarcely exchanging a word. Her long, blonde hair seemed to ripple every time she moved her head.

'Shall I see you tonight?'

'It's difficult, I promised mother I would stay in and do the ironing.'

'Tomorrow, then? There's a good film on at the Scala.'

'All right.'

He was never importunate, there was no need. In any case he liked to think of her taking her place in the home, quietly capable. It proved that she was not like some of the girls at the office who boasted that they could not boil an egg.

When his mother came down stairs it was the signal for another walk. He thought of tramping the five miles across the cliffs to Porthquiddick and catching the bus back. It would be a change, but as he came out on to the quay he was surprised to see his uncle's boat, *Green Lady III*, berthed near the Bray's fish store on the main quay. She was four or five hours early, which meant that there must have been some kind of trouble. There was no sign of *Green Lady*'s crew but Alfie, one of the Bray brothers, was hosing down the cobbles in front of his store.

'Trouble, Alfie?'

'They got their line snagged in an old wreck and lost upwards of a thousand hooks. They're in the loft baiting up and I reckon, if you've nothing better to do, your uncle would be glad of another pair of hands.'

'Any catch?'

'Three stone of whiting, hardly worth going out for.'

A thousand hooks meant half-a-mile of line. When he was younger he had spent a lot of time in his uncle's fish loft, baiting up and, several times, he had gone out long-lining but his mother had disapproved, fearing that he might make fishing his trade.

He made his way back along the quay to the house, changed his clothes, then went to the loft. He found his uncle with two crewmen, sitting on up-turned oil drums, making up a new line.

'Want a hand, uncle?'

His uncle nodded. 'Pull up a drum, Morley. You can give Jimmy a hand with the baiting.'

The loft reeked of tar and fish. Double doors stood open to the quay, framing the brilliant scene outside like a still from a Technicolor film. But the interior of the loft was dimly lit and cool. His uncle and Willie Matthews bent the strops of new hooks to a length of line while Jimmy Tregaskis baited the attached hooks with strips of mackerel. A mackerel was dexterously cut into twenty or thirty pieces and each piece was doubly secured to the hook. His fingers soon became sticky with tar from the line and slippery with blood from the fish but it did not take him long to recover the rhythm of movement which kept the baited line feeding into the basket at his feet.

True to his Tremain stock, his uncle was lean, dark and sallow. He had no moustache but a fringe of black beard along the line of his jaw. A man in his forties, a difficult man and, by all accounts, mean. His crewmen rarely stayed with him for more than a single season and some years he would be looking for a man at the height of the pilchard driving. Often there was trouble over the share-out.

Now and then visitors strolling along the quay stopped to look in and, occasionally, one of them tried to take a photograph in the tricky lighting conditions, but the four men behaved as though they were totally unaware of what was going on.

Willie Matthews was in his second season on the Tremain boat but Jimmy Tregaskis had retired from fishing and had been persuaded to come back for a few weeks to help out. Willie was short, stout and clean shaven with smooth, brown skin which shone as though it had been burnished. Jimmy was wizened, without teeth and he looked out on the world through eyes which were permanently narrowed to slits.

'How's Alice?' Willie Matthews, the stout crewman, his smooth features wrinkled in a smile.

'She's all right.'

'Taking her out tonight?'

'Not tonight.'

'Pretty young maid, sure 'nough.' Jimmy Tregaskis wheezed away over some secret joke. He was a lascivious old man, well known as a Peeping Tom and more than once accused of showing himself to young girls. 'I bet she'll let you put 'n away whenever you have the fancy.'

'None of that, Jimmy!' Harry Tremain turned to glare at the old man. 'You know I'll have none of that talk in my loft.'

Harry Tremain, like most of the family, was a Methodist; he sang in the choir and, occasionally, preached at various chapels round the circuit.

Jimmy said no more and they worked in silence. Their blunt, clumsy-looking fingers never faltered though they rarely looked at the wicked little hooks with their needle-sharp points. By six

14

o'clock they had completed the new line and the two crewmen left. Morley would have gone with them but his uncle called him back.

'Are you serious about this young woman, Morley?'

'I don't know what you mean, uncle.'

His uncle was slow of speech and conversation was always punctuated by long silences.

'You know exactly what I mean. You've got no father and it's my duty to tell you when I see you make a fool of yourself. Those two just now, they were laughing at you, boy.'

'Let them if they want to.'

'That's not the point; they've heard the same gossip as I've heard. The Weekes family are newcomers to the village. They came here, as you know, from Redruth, but the girl's reputation has caught up with her. What surprises me is that your mother hasn't got hold of it, she's usually quick enough. Now if you're thinking of marriage—'

But Morley had turned on his heel and walked out.

That evening he stayed at home with his mother in the upstairs sitting-room, next to his bedroom. He read while his mother knitted. She sat in the bay window watching the harbour which could be seen through a gap in the houses along the front. Monty, their neutered, grey tabby, slept, curled up, on the window-seat. The sky was glowing turquoise, beginning to pale as the sun, hidden behind the houses, dropped to the horizon. The little room was filled with yellow light, evening light, intimate and melancholy. It was so quiet they could hear the footsteps of people walking in the street.

From time to time his mother cleared her throat and made a remark or asked a question, making conversation. He knew that she was preparing the ground, leading up to something. At last it came.

'You're seeing a lot of Alice, aren't you?'

He stiffened. 'I'd have a job not to, seeing she works here.'

'You know what I mean, Morley.'

'We go out sometimes.'

'Do you want to marry her, dear?' She was busy casting off but she stopped to watch his face.

'I'll probably marry her if she'll have me.'

'Have you asked her?'

'No.'

His mother laughed in a patronizing way which he always detested. 'She'll have you all right, Morley, if you give her half a chance. But don't be taken in by that innocent Miss Prim look, she's calculating. That young woman's got her eye on the shop. I'll not deny she's a worker and that's something these days. She's also got the makings of a good head for business, but things like that don't make a marriage, Morley, I should know. If you want my opinion—'

He stood up and threw his book on to the chair. She looked startled. 'What's the matter? Where are you going?'

'Out.' He was incapable of having a row so that his only course was to avoid provocation.

Her voice was tremulous. 'When will you be back?'

'I'll be back.' A grudging concession, part of a bargain which had never been explicitly agreed but always kept. Twelve years before, his father had walked out one evening and never come back. Next morning his body had been found, hanging from a beam in Harry Tremain's fish loft.

Suicide while the balance of his mind was disturbed.

He remembered that evening.

His father and mother had never quarrelled but his mother sometimes nagged with the maddening persistence of a dripping tap. On this occasion his father had walked out and slammed the shop door so that the bell continued to jangle after he had disappeared down the street. Morley remembered too, the next morning, when they heard the news. He had not grieved much because he found it impossible to believe that he would never see his father in the shop again. Now he recalled him as a stranger, a kindly, urbane man, dressed in a long, grey overall, always with a cigarette between his lips. He had a lush black moustache discoloured at the edges by nicotine.

Nineteen forty-two, when the war was at its worst. His father had not been conscripted because of a heart condition.

The sun had set, but in the west the sky was barred by clouds which still glowed orange and red. Elsewhere sky and sea were bleached and it was hard to distinguish any colour among the hulls of the boats in the harbour. Some of them carried feeble mast-head lights. The quays were deserted but as he passed the Robartes Arms he could see, in the bar, a row of men in blue jerseys, sitting motionless as though they were in a chapel pew.

He was upset by what his mother had said but also, paradoxically, relieved. She had not mentioned any gossip and she certainly would have done had she heard it. But she had been clever, it was certainly possible that it was the shop which interested Alice.

He was approaching his uncle's house. Quay House was a gaunt, slate-fronted building at the end of the waterfront. In a lighted room to the right of the front door two of his aunt's boarders, a man and a woman, were seated at the open window, reading. He climbed the steep path, broken by steps, beside the house. The path led up on to the cliff and at the top it divided. He took the left hand fork which ran along the flank of the little promontory bounding the harbour. He knew every inch of the ground and could have walked it blindfolded. The promontory ended in a steep scree with a tumble of rocks below and the western break-water probing out into the sea, a slim, bent finger.

Dusk was giving place to summer darkness and, looking back, the village was a pyramid of lights. He told himself that he could identify the house, the very room in which Alice was at this moment. He could visualize her standing over the ironing board, her head bent, her shoulders slightly hunched as she pressed down the iron.

A sound away to his right attracted his attention, a low moaning sound. He listened and heard it again. There were tricky places where it was easily possible to sustain a nasty fall and he imagined someone lying in pain. He picked his way through the gorse in the direction of the sound and came upon a grassy hollow. He stopped, feeling a fool. A man and a woman lay together, he

17

could see the woman's leg and thigh, pale in the fading light and the moaning was louder, more urgent. He was turning away when he caught sight of her face, white and indescribably tense, her eyes tightly closed, her lips contorted. It was Alice.

For a moment he was incapable of movement and the man became aware of him standing there. The man looked up, half sheepish, half aggressive. There was mutual recognition but neither spoke and Alice remained oblivious. He moved off as quickly as he could, the gorse tearing at his trouser legs.

Alice with his cousin, Cedric.

When he reached the path he ran blindly, taking the fork which led across the cliffs in the direction of Black Head, away from the village. He blundered over a stile and charged down a steep slope, a declivity between two headlands where there was a sandy cove, a favourite spot with those prepared to walk. He ran blindly and, near the bottom of the slope, his foot caught on a gorse root and he fell headlong, spread-eagled on the dry, beaten earth of the path. Never, even in childhood, had he had such a fall—even his face struck the ground; he could feel blood trickling from his nose and he had a stunning pain in his head. Instead of getting up he burst into tears. He could not tell how long he stayed there, shaken with sobs, his cheek against the earth, his fingers clutching as though for dear life.

At last he rolled his body into a sitting position and stood up. He was badly shaken and bruised, his nose still bled and little rivulets of blood ran down his forehead but he could stand and he could walk. He had a sudden unreasoning fear that he might be found there and a desperate longing for the privacy of his own room. He was two miles from the village and it took him three-quarters of an hour to cover the distance. From time to time he stopped, overcome by faintness, and when he reached the water-front the street lamps had been switched off and only the harbour lights shimmered uncertainly across the water. There was no moon and the houses were in darkness. He let himself in by the side door. His mother was waiting for him in the living-room; the clock on the mantelpiece showed a quarter to twelve.

'Morley! What . . . ?'

'I fell down, now don't fuss, mother. Don't fuss, I said!' He shouted, a thing he rarely did and it had its effect. She allowed him to go up to the bathroom and lock himself in. He sat on the toilet seat for a long time, his head in his hands, before he could find the strength to undress. He looked in the mirror; he was a sight, no wonder his mother had been scared. Clotted blood encrusted his forehead, his nostrils and his lips, his eyes were red-rimmed from crying.

He washed gingerly in warm water and patted his cuts and grazes with Dettol. All the time he was conscious of his mother waiting on the landing and twice she plucked up the courage to call,

'Are you all right, Morley?'

When he came out, wearing only his shirt, she was still there.

'Morley, my dear boy!'

But he brushed past her without a word and into his bedroom.

'I'll get you some warm milk and a biscuit . . .'

'No, nothing, I don't want anything.'

The night seemed endless, though he must have slept for at one moment it was dark and the next broad daylight. His body was stiff and sore and the events of the previous evening came back to him like the memory of a bad dream, unnerving, incredible. He listened. The usual sounds, the shop bell, voices. He could not believe that Alice was there, he hoped not. He had decided to behave as though she had never been more than an assistant in his mother's shop. It would be difficult but he had had plenty of practice in doing difficult things. He was dogged and it was doggedness which had got him through the eleven-plus, brought him his modest ordinary level passes and made him useful to his employers.

'How are you feeling, dear?' His mother was standing in the doorway holding a cup of tea. 'I thought you were awake. How do you feel? I looked in on you about five and you were fast asleep then . . .' She fussed over him and made him exasperated.

He asked the question uppermost in his mind. 'Is Alice down there?'

'Alice? Of course she is, dear. I told her you had fallen down and hurt your face and she was upset. I expect she'll be up to see you when things quieten down a bit.'

'I'm getting up.'

'Is that wise, dear?' Her bland smile vanished and she became, suddenly, shrewd. 'This fall, dear, was it something to do with Alice?'

'Of course not, don't be absurd, mother.'

She seemed to accept that, but he would have to be careful.

He spent the morning in the dining-room pretending to read, lacking the courage to go into the shop. At eleven o'clock his mother came in to make a pot of tea. She drank hers, standing by the window, watching the passers-by. Then she went back to the shop, calling as she went, 'I'll send Alice in.'

'No!' But she had gone.

He braced himself and a moment later Alice came in, looking the same as ever, her eyes, for once, expressive, full of concern.

'I wanted to come before but I haven't had a minute. What on earth happened, Morley? How did you do it?'

Yet she must have heard him blundering off through the undergrowth. What had Cedric said to her?

'Some bloody snooper.'

She was standing close to his chair, one hand on his shoulder, her breast brushing his cheek, her smell in his nostrils. 'Poor old boy, what rotten luck.'

He waited until he was sure that his voice would not let him down then he said, slowly and deliberately, 'I don't want to see you again, Alice.'

She seemed not to understand. 'What do you mean? You don't want to see me again, have I done something to upset you?'

She sounded so surprised and so sincere that, for a moment, he almost doubted the evidence of his own eyes, but he merely said, 'If you don't know what I'm talking about you'd better ask

Cedric.' He could feel tears smarting in his eyes but he contrived to keep his voice steady.

She drew away with a little laugh. 'What are you on about?' She sounded false now and it hurt him more than a brazen admission would have done.

'Just go away and leave me alone.'

'Alice!' His mother's voice from the shop.

She hesitated. 'I've got to go now, but I'll be back. Whatever it is you've heard, I can explain.'

'Don't bother, it would be a waste of time.'

It gave him a bitter satisfaction to treat her with contempt. But when she had gone he gave way to uncontrollable sobbing. When the fit had passed he bathed his eyes under the kitchen tap and decided that he could not bear being cooped up in the house all day. After examining his face in the mirror over the dining-room mantelpiece he went through to the shop and, ignoring Alice, said to his mother, 'I'm going out.'

'Do you think you should?'

'I think I'll drop in on Aunt Clara and Eunice.'

She looked at him sharply, for his visits to the slate-fronted house on the quay were rare and he always needed persuasion.

'Well, if you're really going there you could take your uncle's papers. Get Uncle Harry's papers, Alice.'

Alice went into the back room and returned with a *Mirror* and a *Mail*. She handed him the papers and their fingers touched. Her expression was enigmatic as always.

He walked along the quay, keeping his head averted from passers-by. He felt that he had to talk to somebody and though his aunt and Eunice would pry, it would be better than the tense, emotionally-charged atmosphere at home.

There was a whole flight of granite steps up to his uncle's front door because the ground floor was level, not with the quay, but with the grassy slopes of the promontory behind. The front door stood open to a stone-flagged passage. Morley went in without knocking, down the passage to the kitchen. His Aunt Clara, in a floral pinafore, was cutting up meat for pasties while a plump, ginger cat clawed the leg of the table in almost frantic greed.

Aunt Clara was lean, angular and waspish. Apart from Cedric, who was twenty-one, she had a daughter, Eunice, twenty and growing daily more like her mother.

'Oh, it's you. What on earth have you done to your face?'

'I brought the papers, aunt.'

'So I see. I asked you what you've done to your face. You look like you've been in a fight.'

'I fell down.'

'Some fall!' His aunt had started to chip little piles of potato. 'How's your mother?'

'All right. I suppose uncle was away early this morning?'

'Fiveish. There's no fish about and, as you know, they lost part of a line yesterday.' She pursed her thin lips. 'If things don't pick up we shan't cover the boat and the gear this season.'

According to Aunt Clara nothing the Harry Tremains touched ever made money though it was known that they were better off than any family in the village.

There were slow, clumping footsteps on the stairs and a little grey-haired woman came in. She wore a black wrap-over pinafore, grey stockings wrinkled around her ankles and slippers which flip-flopped as she walked.

'I've done the beds, Clara. Shall I do the stairs or do you want me to wash up first?'

Clara went on chipping potatoes and did not bother to look up but she said, aggressively, 'There's no point in washing up till I've finished, is there?'

Ella Jordan was said to be Clara's half-sister but nobody seemed very sure of the exact nature of the relationship. There was something of a mystery about her—for one thing she was a Catholic in a family which had been Methodist since Wesley. Now she was just a poor relation and her only vanity was the little gold crucifix which she always wore round her neck.

'All right, I'll do the stairs.' She went out and Clara's eyes followed her.

'As if I hadn't got enough to put up with.' She had finished the potatoes and started on turnip; the little piles of meat and vegetables were growing. 'Still on holiday then?'

'I've got a few more days.'

His aunt made a clicking noise with her tongue. 'I can't remember the last time I had a holiday.'

The kitchen was almost unbearably hot because the Cornish range had been stoked up to baking heat. The coals glowed fiercely between the bars and a shower of fine, hot ash filtered down into the iron drawer with its big brass knob. Despite the heat, great-grandfather Tremain, who was ninety-eight, sat, as usual, in his old Windsor chair, close to the range. He was so much a part of the kitchen that nobody seemed to notice him. His skin, like mottled parchment, was tight on his shrunken bones and he sat, hands resting on thin thighs, staring at the fire without moving a muscle. He wore a peaked cap and blue jersey as he had done when he put to sea in *Green Lady II*. His son, Morley's grandfather, had lost his life in a minesweeper in the first war but it was Clara's intention to keep the old man alive until he reached a hundred and received a telegram from the new Queen.

Clara was looking at Morley critically. 'Your face is a sight and no mistake. You look like somebody gave you a good hiding.'

'I told you, aunt, I fell down.'

'I know what you told me, I'm not deaf nor daft.'

'Where's Eunice?'

'Gone to the shops. I told her to collect the papers but now you've brought them.'

'Many in?' He tried to keep the conversation on non-controversial matters for, if he left, he would be forced back on himself.

'Five, two couples and a single.' She brushed back a wisp of hair with her forearm. 'Two more couples coming Saturday.'

There was silence for a while as she rolled out the dough for the pasties.

'I don't know how they manage at that office of yours without you. To listen to your mother, you'd think they couldn't spare you for a single day, let alone a fortnight.'

23

Cedric worked as a fitter's mate at the stone quarry down the coast and she could never forgive her nephew for having an office job which she regarded as carrying superior status.

The back door was open and beyond the little patch of walled-in garden, the land rose steeply in a natural rockery with sedums and thrift growing in the sparse soil between outcrops of lichen-encrusted granite. The cliff path ran along farther up and a young couple were walking along it, arms round each other, lost. They brought a lump to his throat.

There were steps in the passage and Eunice came in carrying a string-bag full of groceries. She was thin like most of the Tremains, pale, with lifeless skin. Her forehead bulged over her eyes and seemed to be permanently speckled with little beads of sweat. She wore spectacles with small, oval lenses which accentuated her broad features. She acknowledged her cousin curtly without looking at him properly.

'Still on holiday?'

He did not answer and she looked up. 'God! What have you done to your face?'

They had grown up together, like brother and sister, until he was twelve or thirteen, then they had drifted apart. When she was seventeen and Morley was already working at the clay works, she had made a determined effort to renew their association. For half a year they went about together and the village assumed that a match was in the making. The Harry Tremains looked with favour on events which would give them a possible foothold in the shop. But the idea of marriage to Eunice had never entered Morley's head, he would as soon have thought of marrying a sister.

Morley read a lot, almost anything he could get from the library or buy in paperbacks and he liked to talk about what he read. Eunice listened with exemplary patience but her contributions always surprised him by their almost wilful banality. He did his best to educate her but it was an unprofitable task. Then, one summer evening, when they were sitting on Black Head watching the boats creep home, Eunice decided to take a hand in his education. Her attempt, inexpert and crude, only puzzled and

24

embarrassed him. Solemn-eyed and frowning he had taken both her hands in his and said, 'I don't think you know what you are doing, Uny, dear.'

Eunice, angry and humiliated, had complained to her mother that Morley had assaulted her and she was even more bitterly hurt when her mother replied with a soothing platitude. Since that time the couple had seen little of each other except at family gatherings and, when they did meet, Eunice did her best to put him in his place.

She opened the brown leather purse she was carrying and started to count out the change. 'I couldn't get any pork sausages, only beef. It came to one pound and fivepence and here's your change, nineteen and sevenpence out of two pound.'

She turned to Morley. 'Throwing your money about Monday evening, wasn't you? Front row of the circle at the Odeon with that Alice Weekes. Proper little madam she is. I hope you know what you're doing there.'

As always he felt bound to justify himself, however absurdly. 'We saw the film of the Coronation in colour. It was very good.'

Eunice sniffed. 'I know, I was there. You see the same film even in the cheap seats.'

There was an uncomfortable silence, then he said, 'I was wondering if you are going to the carnival on Saturday?'

She looked at him sharply. 'Is that an invitation?'

'Yes.'

She was taken aback and even her mother looked at him in surprise.

'Are you serious?'

'Of course.'

'All right, then.'

'I'll call for you about five, then we can watch the judging.'

Eunice went as far as the front door with him and her manner was quite different; warm and friendly.

'See you Saturday, then.'

Chapter Two

NEXT DAY THE weather had changed, the sky was uniformly grey and there was a strong wind blowing from the south with a promise of more to come. The sea was leaden with streaks of brilliant white foam and even in the basin waves slapped against the quay and the smaller craft bobbed about to a crazy rhythm. Now and then heavier clouds, chased by the wind, brought squalls of stinging rain. The boats had not gone out because of the weather and their crews were gathered in the lofts.

Morley could not face a day indoors; in any case he had decided on a bold front. People would believe any version of how he had come by his bruises except the true one. Let them! Since childhood he had been accustomed to being an outsider. Unpopular at school, often the butt of his classmates, he had contrived a screen round himself, an emotional screen which isolated him from many things which might otherwise have shocked or disturbed him. He put on his mackintosh, buttoned to the neck, and went down to the harbour.

The basin was crowded with small craft almost jostling each other. In the outer harbour the green hull of Uncle Harry's *Green Lady III* stood out, as always, among the blues of the fishing boats and the white launches. Green was supposed to be an unlucky colour but for some reason lost to memory the Tremain boats had always been called by the same name and painted green—pea-green. It was one of the things which helped to mark off the Tremains from other families, they were different and the unnatural colour of their boat was a symbol of that difference.

Morley walked along the eastern edge of the basin, past Alec Martin's little cafe and a ramshackle shed occupied by an emaciated, red-bearded painter. The painter used the front of the shed as a studio and slept in the back behind a bead curtain. A succession of nubile girls had shared his shed and his bed over the two years he had been there, providing the village with a rare opportunity to be entertained and scandalized with little sense of guilt. Where the girls came from or where they went nobody knew. For a week or two the painter's gangling figure would be seen of a morning mooching round the shops then, abruptly, he would be replaced by some dusky girl (they were all dark), carrying his string bag and wearing a skimpy dress and sandals or with bare feet. Morley's uncle had had his portrait done by the painter.

As Morley passed, the painter was standing in his doorway staring gloomily at the lowering sky and smoking his long-stemmed clay pipe. He acknowledged Morley with a nod and Morley was continuing on his way to the outer harbour when he heard his name called. To his annoyance he saw that it was Cedric. Cedric aboard *Green Lady III*, in the act of stepping into the dinghy.

'Hang on, Morley!' Standing in the dinghy Cedric pulled himself ashore, hand over hand, by a mooring rope hitched to a ring on the quay.

All through Morley's childhood and youth his cousin, Cedric, had been held up to him as a warning. 'You're getting more like your cousin every day!' or 'I can see Cedric in you!' The strongest censures in his mother's repertoire. Cedric had been and still was grossly indulged by his mother who lavished on him all the love of which she was capable and Cedric had reacted dramatically from the first. At eight he had been before the juvenile court for stealing, at ten he was there for viciously attacking another boy with a length of mooring chain. After that he had kept out of the courts, but only just. When he was fourteen he had caused a sensation by kicking and punching a young woman teacher at the village school. Only the fact that his father was a school manager had enabled the incident to be hushed up. From school he had been apprenticed at the clay works but he had been sacked after a year. Now he was a fitter's mate at the stone quarry and he seemed to have achieved a precarious equilibrium.

Overlooking his exploits with girls there had been no real scandal for a long time.

Cedric reached the iron ladder, secured the painter of the dinghy and climbed on to the quay. He wiped his hands on a piece of oily cotton-waste and stuffed it into his pocket.

'The old man asked me to have a look at the timing on the Kelvin.'

Cedric's greatest detractors could never deny his skill as a mechanic although he had not learned the trade in any formal manner. He was a natural with engines and gadgets and he lavished loving care on the motor cycle which enabled him to spread his reputation as a rogue male far and wide in the county.

He stared at Morley's bruised face. 'They told me you was in trouble, what you been doing to yourself, mate?'

'I fell down.'

It sounded improbable and Cedric looked incredulous but all he said was, 'Christ!'

'Not working today?' Morley tried to keep his end up but he was uneasy. It was not unknown for Cedric, after a longish period with no contact, to make a friendly approach but in view of what had happened . . .

'I'm on tonight,' Cedric said, 'due in at seven. Two hours kip this afternoon will see me right. The big crusher's in need of overhaul and they can't afford to shut down by day. Overtime rates so why worry?'

Cedric was a year younger than Morley, sturdier, stockier, a coarser version of the Tremain breed, and Morley always felt like a child in his company. Despite his lamentable past and his exploits with girls, perhaps because of them, he was accepted as a man, an equal with his father and the other fishermen, on the same footing as the quarrymen and those who travelled to the clay works on an earlier bus than Morley.

'The old man asked me to take a look at the timing on the Kelvin . . . Two hours kip this afternoon will see me right . . .' At

28

such times Morley did not feel so complacent about his office job and his blue blazer with the brass buttons. He was still, for too many people, the Tremain boy at the shop.

Turning back along the quay they were caught in one of the sudden rain squalls. The wind stiffened so that they had to lie back against it, then the rain whip-lashed across the harbour, hissing down, flattening the waves and cutting visibility to a few yards. They passed the painter's shack but he had gone inside and closed his door.

Outside the Robartes Arms Cedric said, 'Feel like a drink before dinner?'

Morley rarely went into a bar but he could not bring himself to part from Cedric until he had heard all there was to hear.

'If you like.'

The public bar belonged to the locals; in bad weather they used it as an alternative to the fish lofts and it had a family atmosphere. Any tourist who intruded soon realized his mistake and took his custom to the other bar. Now at mid-day there were several customers, the windows were steamed up and the air was heavy with tobacco smoke.

As they went in there was a murmur of greeting but Morley knew that it was for his cousin, not for him. For most of the men in the bar he was as much an outsider as any tourist.

'What's up then, Ceddie, got the sack?'

'They've found the bugger out, that's what it is.'

'Caught him with his fingers in the bloody nuts and bolts.'

Cedric, unperturbed, went to the bar. 'Usual for me, Matt. What about you, Morley?'

'I'll have a half.' He knew that they were eyeing him, looking at his bruised face and speculating, but he also knew that they would say nothing. To do so would be to acknowledge him as one of them.

Cedric collected the drinks and carried them to a table near one of the windows, away from the rest of the company.

'Cheers.'

'Cheers.'

Cedric wiped his lips with the back of his hand. 'It was unlucky Wednesday night, Morley, old boy.'

'Unlucky?'

'You coming along like you did.'

Morley had unbuttoned his mackintosh and wiped his glasses. Despite himself he was impressed. Instead of keeping out of his way, hoping that he had not been recognized, here was Cedric, brazening it out, preparing to have a cosy chat over a glass of beer.

'You weren't following us, were you?'

'Certainly not!'

Cedric nodded. 'There you are, then. Like I said, unlucky.' He pulled out a crushed packet of Woodbines and lit one.

Morley sipped his beer self-consciously and waited.

'I just wanted to find out how we stood. I mean, we don't want to get our wires crossed, not in the family.' He broke off, confronted by Morley's unwinking stare. 'I mean, you wasn't serious about her, was you, Morley?' He looked incredulous as though the remote possibility had just occurred to him.

'Yes.' The word seemed to be forced from his lips.

'But she's a scrubber, mate. You don't want to get serious with the likes of her. Her old man moved here from Redruth to find some place where they wasn't known. The trouble is the poor old bugger didn't move far enough. The lads at the quarry know all about Alice, believe you me!' He looked genuinely concerned. 'You mustn't be taken in by that china-doll look, Morley.' He used a particularly crude expression to make his point.

Morley flushed but said nothing.

Cedric eyed him with curiosity and impatience. 'Well, I'm only telling you for your own good, mate; it's no skin off my nose. Granted she's not bad to look at but when it comes to anything more than hit an' run . . .'

It was incredible. Somehow they had reached a position where he was expected to be grateful. And in an odd way, he was. In Cedric's company, in this sort of atmosphere, he came near to recognizing a system of values altogether different from his own, less demanding, offering a greater freedom. At that moment he was not angry with his cousin but envious. He could recall Alice's white face and the quickening rhythm of her moans without disgust. He could have been there in Cedric's place if . . . If what? Sometimes it seemed to him that he did not live in the real world but in some world of make-believe which he had constructed from his own imaginings.

'Will you have another?'

Cedric grinned. 'Now you're talking.'

When he left the bar he had had enough to feel elevated and his problems seemed to have shrunk to manageable proportions. The rain had stopped, a few visitors had ventured on to the pier-heads where they were being drenched with salt spray; others, in raincoats, were mooning about the quays. He was almost blown along by the wind at his back and as he walked his lips kept forming the words, 'You've got to come to terms . . .'

The shop was shut for the lunch hour and Alice had gone home. His mother was in the living-room watching for him from the window.

'Are you all right, Morley? I've been that worried! Do you know it's two o'clock? I've got to open the shop in fifteen minutes.'

For lunch on weekdays they always had something easy to prepare, today it was tinned salmon with salad. The pink fish and the slightly sickly odour turned his stomach.

'I don't want any lunch.'

She looked at him sharply. 'Have you been drinking?'

In the afternoon the wind strengthened to a full gale, the squalls came more frequently and by the time the shop closed there was no question of going anywhere except in emergency. He spent another evening in the upstairs sitting-room with his mother, reading and listening to the radio while the gale roared outside. From the window they could see a broad segment of the bay, a grey turmoil of sea and sky and, every fifteen minutes or so, a darker wall of mist marked the advance of yet another squall as it raced towards the shore. At nine o'clock the wind was at its peak but by midnight it had almost died away.

Morley lay awake until the early hours, then he must have fallen asleep. When he awoke it was half-past eight on a fine, fresh morning.

He had his breakfast then delivered his uncle's papers, had a word with Eunice and afterwards went for a walk on the cliffs.

He was observing himself as one might do after an illness, prescribing treatment and estimating the progress of recovery. Asking Eunice to go with him to the carnival was part of the treatment. For one thing he needed company. All the same he was pleased with his progress. He had gone the right way about it by making it a task to be done, like passing an examination.

He called for Eunice just before five o'clock and found the family at tea. Because of the carnival none of the boats had put to sea and Harry Tremain was there with his family. He sat at the head of the table in the kitchen with Cedric on his right, Eunice on his left and his wife opposite him. Ella Jordan had a place laid next to Eunice but most of the time she hovered, ready to cut more bread and butter, pour tea or remove dirty plates. Tea was the last meal of the day and it was always substantial, ham and tongue or fried fish followed by home made 'splits' with jam and cream topped off with a slice or two of saffron cake and washed down with several cups of strong tea.

Morley's reception was cordial and he was aware at once that a new situation had been recognized and approved. For a moment he felt trapped, but he needed human contacts and soon his misgivings melted away in the warmth of his welcome.

'Pour Morley a cup of tea, Ella.'

'Here, have one of these, Morley,' and he was given a plate on which there was a split loaded with jam and cream.

'But I've had tea . . .'

'You can't fatten a Tremain, except for Cedric here, I don't know who he takes after.'

Eunice was wearing a sleeveless frock with orange, white and brown stripes, and she had done something to her hair so that it seemed to have bounce instead of hanging lankly round her thin face. Seen from behind she had a certain appeal, her thin, white arms made him feel protective. If only her forehead . . .

Soon she left the table and went upstairs to get ready. When she came down she was wearing a light-weight mustard-coloured coat which he had not seen before and he thought that she looked smart.

'Have a good time. We'll leave the door on the latch.'

'Don't do anything I wouldn't,' from Cedric.

'None of that talk, Cedric!' from his father.

Morley felt vaguely uncomfortable, they were rushing him.

Outside on the quay Eunice put her hand in his; her thin, bony fingers were moist. They went up into the main street and along the street to the square. There was a general movement in that direction and they joined the stream. In the square they turned off up the hill to the recreation ground where the judging was being held. About twenty floats and fifty or sixty walking entrants, some with prams or barrows, were drawn up in a circle like a pioneering waggon-train and the judges were making their solemn circuit, writing in their books. In the grandstand a brass band was playing. Near the gate a cluster of vans with drop-down sides were selling snacks, ices, rock and nougat.

'Aren't you going to buy me some nougat?'

He had forgotten her insatiable appetite. Before they left the ground she would have consumed, not only the nougat, but probably an ice and something from the snack bar also. But what did it matter? He had his arm round her and it was possible to imagine a comely body under the thin material of her summer coat.

'Morley, what happened about Alice?'

'That's all over.'

'Did you find out about her?'

'I don't want to talk about it.'

She pressed against him affectionately.

Although there were a lot of people they were spread over a large space and tended to cluster into groups. His eyes wandered ceaselessly over the groups looking for, yet fearing to see, Alice's golden head among them.

When the judging was over the procession formed up with the band at its head and set out to tour the village. They climbed on to the hedge to watch the march out of the field and the band was already in the square when the last entry left the ground.

'Do you want to see it again?'

She looked up at him, frowning. 'It's up to you.'

The spectators were straggling out of the ground and down the hill.

'Let's go for a walk.'

That afternoon, for the first time in his life, he had gone to the chemist's shop in the square and bought contraceptives. Now the very thought of them in his pocket made him feel uncomfortably hot; it was not a pleasant sensation. They turned up the hill away from the village.

People were coming down the hill in twos and threes on their way to the village from the new houses and, too late, he spotted Alice with her father and mother. They gave him a pleasant good evening and Alice looked at him with the same calm, expressionless face as always.

'Bitch!' Eunice said under her breath. 'That gave her something to think about anyway.'

They continued up the hill, past the council houses where Alice lived. Beyond the council houses they followed a narrow lane leading off to the left, an avenue arched over by elms. A stream ran in a ditch by the road and ferns grew so luxuriantly that it was almost impossible to see the dark water. Eunice stopped and held up her lips to be kissed. He stooped to kiss her and she thrust her body hard against his.

A little way along the lane a field gate stood open and, just inside the field, there was an open barn with the remnants of last year's straw. She guided him in, he spread the coat he had been carrying on the straw and they sat down. The sun was still warm and shone straight into the shed. The field sloped away steeply so that their view was bounded by a vast expanse of sea. Eunice had her hand inside his shirt and one of the buttons flew off. For a time they lay together in an embrace which was not only uncomfortable but painful.

'You remember the last time?'

'Yes.' In fact he was trying hard to get it out of his mind.

'You're a big boy now.'

He felt that he must do something so he slipped his hand under her dress and let it rest on her thigh.

'Do you want to?'

He said, 'Yes.'

She sat up. 'Have you got anything? If you haven't I expect it will be all right.'

'I have.'

She seemed surprised. 'If you're shy, you can go over there.'

When he came back she had taken off her coat and she was lying on her back with one leg slightly raised. Light from the low sun was kind to her pallid skin and she had taken off her glasses. For the first time he truly desired her. Her dress buttoned down the front and she started undoing the buttons, beginning at the top. He bent over her, trembling. She reached the last button then, with an odd little smile, she whisked open her dress. She was completely naked underneath.

He did not move but continued to stare at her, though now his emotions had totally changed. Her thin, white body, her breasts scarcely more developed than a boy's, her legs like sticks and the little fuzzy brown triangle of her sex repelled him yet, at the same time, seemed to invite his compassion. His final emotion was one of tenderness a million miles removed from sex.

The next few minutes were the most humiliating he had ever experienced. Her coaxing gave way to anger and her anger flared into vituperation. She used words which had never passed his lips and which he had supposed no decent girl would know.

Chapter Three

I T   W A S   S U N D A Y. The day had been fine until late afternoon when the sky had clouded over and it had started to rain. Now, at chapel-time, the village was drenched in an unrelenting drizzle. The narrow streets were alive with people on their way to chapel under a canopy of umbrellas and Morley's mother was one of them. The boats had been in harbour all day for there was no Sunday fishing from the port and the men, in black suits, either went to chapel with their wives or to the Robartes Arms.

Morley's mother followed her usual Sunday routine. When she returned from chapel she changed out of her tailored costume into a grey, linen working dress and, for an hour and a half, sitting at a desk in the room behind the shop, she worked on her accounts. People passing to and from the harbour could look in and see her, perched on a stool, making out bills or entering figures in a ledger. Sarah Pascoe. As a girl she had attended the village school and a good many men of the village remembered casting an appraising eye over her when she was a pretty, blonde school-girl with freckles. But she had always behaved in a manner older than her years and when they tried to flirt with her she made them feel small. In the end she had become Sarah Tremain and people said that she had married the shop.

At half-past nine she put her books away and went to the foot of the stairs.

'What would you like for supper, Morley?'

'I don't want any supper.'

'There's some lamb left, I could make you a sandwich.'

'No thanks, I don't want anything.'

She climbed the stairs and went to his bedroom to find him, fully dressed, lying on his bed.

'Is there something wrong, Morley?'

'What? No, nothing. I'm just not hungry.'

'But you had no tea.'

'I had a big lunch.'

She stood, watching him, trying to think of something she could say which might move him to confide in her.

'Is it Alice?'

'Is what Alice? I don't know what you're talking about.'

She persisted, doggedly.

'You haven't been going out together this last few days.'

'Haven't we?'

'I saw her mother in chapel.'

He did not answer and she changed her ground again.

'What about a cup of cocoa or a glass of milk?'

'I don't want anything, mother.' The irritation in his voice warned her not to push him any further.

At a little before eleven she went up to bed. The door of his room was open and she looked in. He seemed to be asleep and he had undressed, for his clothes were arranged on a chair by the window. She closed the door gently.

She had dozed off when she was awakened by a bell ringing. At first she thought it was the alarm clock by her bed then she realized that it was the side-door bell. She switched on the light. A quarter to one. She got up, pulled on a dressing-gown over her nightdress, felt for her slippers and put them on. She caught sight of herself in the wardrobe mirror and thought of stopping to remove her curlers but decided not to.

The side door opened off a tiny hall. The bolts were stiff and she had to rotate them back and forth before they would draw. Whoever it was had stopped ringing the bell.

It was dark in the narrow street and raining hard. There were two men at the door; one of them was George Price, the police constable, but she did not recognize the other. He was short and stout, wearing a mackintosh and a cloth cap.

'Sorry to get you out of bed, Sarah. This is Mr Weekes, Alice's father.' George Price had been at school with Sarah but she had

37

not met Alice's father, though she had heard that he suffered from asthma.

'Come in, do, out of this terrible rain.'

George Price seemed to fill the little hall and his waterproof dripped on to the tiled floor.

'Alice hasn't come home and her parents are worried.'

Weekes was breathing hard and his face was flushed. 'We haven't seen her since she went out right after dinner.'

Sarah switched on the light in the dining-room and they followed her in. The table was laid for breakfast and the dishes were covered with a striped cloth.

George Price took off his helmet and brushed droplets of water from his moustache. 'I thought Morley might have seen her, they've been about together a fair bit lately.'

'Morley hasn't been outside the door since tea.' Sarah was on the defensive.

'He could have seen her this afternoon.'

Weekes was breathing rapidly through his mouth and he seemed to be leaning against the sideboard for support.

'Are you all right, Mr Weekes?'

He put out his hand as though to ward off any concern. 'I'm all right ma'am, I'm asthmatic and when I'm a bit flustered ... It's nothing.'

'Perhaps a drop of brandy?'

'No, thank you, ma'am, I never touch spirits.' He straightened up. 'I'm sorry to bring our troubles to your door, ma'am, but my wife is very worried.'

Nobody had heard Morley come down the stairs; now he stood in the doorway, knotting the cord of his dressing-gown. He was even paler than usual and his eyes behind his spectacles looked enormous.

'Is something wrong?'

His mother explained and he listened without any change of expression. 'I expect she'll turn up all right.'

'What makes you say that?' Price's manner was sharp.

Morley addressed himself to the girl's father. 'Well, it isn't the first time, is it, Mr Weekes?'

Weekes looked at him in surprise, his laboured breathing ceased for a moment as a dog stops panting. 'Did she tell you?'

'No, I heard it from outside.'

'Is that why you stopped seeing her?'

Morley's manner was less assured. 'I suppose so.'

Weekes nodded. 'We thought there was something.' He turned to Sarah who was standing, tight-lipped, looking from one to the other. 'We had a bit of trouble with Alice before we came here.'

'What sort of trouble?'

Weekes hesitated. 'She got mixed up in the wrong company and she was beginning to lead a wild sort of life. We thought that in a new place she could make a fresh start and when she came to work for you and was going out with Morley we . . . well, we hoped and believed that she was settling down.' He picked up his cap from the chair. 'I'm very sorry to have been the cause of getting you both from your beds.'

He moved out into the hall but Price stayed where he was. 'That's all very well, but Alice is still missing, Morley. When did you last go out with her?'

'On Tuesday evening.'

'You haven't seen her since?'

'Only in the shop.'

'Was she going out with anybody else?'

'Probably.' His manner was sullen.

'You stopped going out with her because you had heard a rumour that she was a bit wild, is that right?'

'It was more than a rumour.'

'You went out this afternoon?'

'I went out alone, yes.'

'Do you mind telling me where?'

'I walked to Drum Point and back.'

'And you didn't see Alice?'

'I've already told you.'

39

'You've no idea where she might be or who she might be with?'

'Unless she's out with Cedric.'

'Cedric? Has she been going out with Cedric?'

'You'd better ask him.'

George Price looked as though he would answer aggressively but changed his mind. He apologized, in his turn, for getting them out of bed and left with Weekes. Sarah bolted the door behind them.

'You should have told me.'

'There was nothing to tell.'

Sarah pulled her dressing-gown round her and shivered. 'Well, you'd better get back to bed, you've got to go to work in the morning.'

When he was half way up the stairs she called after him. 'You would tell me if you knew anything, wouldn't you, Morley?'

He stopped on the stair without turning. 'About what?'

She could not keep the irritation from her voice. 'About Alice, of course.'

'I don't know anything, why should I?'

In the morning he was back to his usual routine. The alarm went off at a quarter to seven and at a few minutes to eight he passed through the shop where his mother was opening up. The bus driver had dropped the parcel of papers in the doorway five minutes before and the bus was now waiting in the square at the end of the street. Often, on his way to the bus, he would pass Alice going to work, but not this morning.

It was a fine morning but the wind was still in a rainy quarter and showers were forecast.

The bus driver was lolling against the radiator of his bus smoking a cigarette.

'Back to the grind, Morley?'

Usually it annoyed him to be addressed in this familiar way by the driver but this morning he did not notice.

'Good holiday?'

'Yes, thanks.'

40

He was wearing a grey suit with a fine stripe and he carried his briefcase and an umbrella.

There were three or four other regulars on the bus already and he took his usual seat, on the left of the gangway, second from the front. The regulars asked him about his holiday and made wisecracks about his face.

'Glad to be back?'

'What do you think?'

He responded to the usual banter absentmindedly. From his seat he could look up the hill, the way Alice came to work; he could see, also, along the main street, now completely blocked by vans unloading.

He was on edge, like a rabbit who senses danger but is unable to decide from which direction the threat comes. He was half expecting to see George Price, the policeman, making his way between the parked vans, half expecting that he would come to the bus to say . . . To say what?

The driver climbed into his seat and started the engine. Two girls, always late, came running across the square and got in just as the bus was pulling away. They climbed the hill out of the village in bottom gear, grinding and shuddering. At the end of Alice's road they stopped to pick up another girl, a plump, fluffy blonde who worked as an assistant in one of the draper's shops in the town. Morley had scarcely spoken half a dozen words to her before but this morning she came and sat beside him taking more than half the seat. Her thigh pressed against his and he was aware of the smell of stale sweat not altogether hidden by the scent she used.

'I suppose you know about Alice?'

'What about her?' It seemed that his whole body ceased to function while he waited for the girl's answer.

'She didn't come home last night and now they've organized a search.'

'A search?'

'They've sent police in and my father, who's an auxiliary coastguard, has been asked to help.'

41

'A search,' he repeated stupidly with no intention or meaning.

She looked at him, puzzled. 'Apparently somebody saw her on the cliffs yesterday afternoon and nobody has seen her since.' She took a cigarette from her handbag and lit it. 'I'm surprised they didn't come to you first off.'

They had reached the top of the hill and were threading their way through a maze of lanes.

'Who saw her?'

'I don't know who saw her but they say it was along the Top Path.'

The top path led to an old mine-working high on the cliffs to the west of the village, Drum Point was to the east.

Morley left the bus on the outskirts of the town and walked to the office where he worked. He hung his raincoat and umbrella in the cloak-room, signed the staff-book and walked down the passage to the cubicle which he shared with two girls. It was his job, and the girls helped him, to check time sheets against the record from the punch-clocks and to prepare summary sheets.

'Morley has to authorize every penny they pay in wages, thousands every week.' This was his mother's version and it was true that his initials appeared at the bottom of each summary sheet. The clock records for the previous Friday and for weekend working were already on his desk and he settled to work. At a few minutes after nine the two girls joined him and after they had teased him about his injured face normal routine was established. Before long it almost seemed that he had not been away, his fears had been resolutely thrust into the back of his mind, but, now and then, he was suddenly possessed by them and suffered acute, physical distress so that he might easily have been sick.

At twelve o'clock, John Collins, his boss, came in from next door.

'Mr Marsh wants to see you in his office right away, Morley.'

Mr Marsh was the chief accountant and interviews with him meant that, for good or ill, something important was in the wind.

The two girls looked at him curiously; for them he was an un-known quantity, a bit stuck up and a bit wet but that sort often got on. He put on his jacket, straightened his tie and ran a comb through his hair. It never crossed his mind that the summons might have anything to do with Alice. He even had a wild thought that it might be about a vacancy he knew to be imminent two steps up the ladder from his present job.

He made his way through the corridors to the executive offices and knocked on a door labelled Chief Accountant.

Mr Marsh's secretary was grey-haired and superior; she scarcely looked up. 'Mr Marsh is expecting you, you may go right through.'

Mr Marsh was at his desk, facing the door, but sitting with his back to Morley was a uniformed policeman.

'There you are, Tremain! Come in. This is Constable Paynter.'

He stood in the doorway, unable to move, frightened that he might faint. The constable stood up and faced him, he was not much older than Morley but stockily built.

'Mr Tremain? You're wanted down at the station, sir. I've got a car outside.'

'The station?'

'They want your help with some enquiries they are making, sir. You'll have it explained to you when you get there.'

Morley looked at Mr Marsh who was swivelling his chair first one way then the other, waiting for them to go.

'Better go along, Tremain, get it sorted out, whatever it is.'

He had had time to pull himself together. 'I'll get my coat.'

'No need, sir, I'll bring you back in the car.'

A morsel of reassurance.

The police car was drawn up on the gravel outside the executive offices and Morley got into the back with Constable Paynter. There was a uniformed driver.

He had to ask, 'What's happened?'

The constable's manner changed now that Mr Marsh was no longer there. 'No good asking us, mate, we're only messenger boys.'

The police station was an old, granite building near the town centre but there were huts behind and it was to one of these that he was taken. A room with a counter and a sergeant behind it.

'Mr Tremain? Just sit over there, please. You'll not be kept waiting very long.'

But he was kept waiting for twenty minutes. Then a constable he had not seen before took him along a passage into a cubicle with a table and two chairs.

'Just wait here a minute or two.'

Another quarter of an hour. Had they found Alice? What would they ask him? He tried to remember the questions Constable Price had asked and the answers he had given. He must keep a tight hold, somehow control this trembling in the stomach... Vitally important to think before saying anything. Vitally important...

A youngish man in a lounge suit came in and took the chair opposite him. The constable who had brought him there stood just inside the door.

'Mr Morley Tremain? Just one or two questions.'

'What about?'

'My name is Martin, Detective Inspector Martin.' He took some papers from a briefcase and sorted them through. 'Now then, I think you told Constable Price that you went for a walk yesterday afternoon. Is that right?'

'Yes.'

'Good. In the direction of Drum Point?'

'Yes.'

He had hesitated for a split second and the inspector looked at him with shrewd eyes. 'You are quite sure?'

'Yes.'

'Drum Point is to the east of the village?'

'Yes, up the coast.' He added, after a moment, 'Hasn't she come home yet?'

The inspector looked at him blankly. 'I'll ask the questions, Mr Tremain.' He referred to his papers again.

The little room was part of a prefabricated hut, the walls were bare concrete and the metal-framed windows were fitted with frosted glass. Morley could hear the traffic on a nearby road but though he knew the town so well he could not locate the road. He felt entirely cut off.

'When was the last time you went out with Alice Weekes?'

'On Tuesday evening.'

'Were you in love with her?'

'I thought I was.'

'Then why did you suddenly stop going out with her?'

He shifted uncomfortably on his hard seat. 'I found out about her.'

'What did you find out?'

'That she would go with anybody.'

'How did you find that out?'

'My uncle told me.'

'And you believed him—just like that?'

'He had no reason to lie.'

'Did you have it out with her?'

'No.' He hesitated then added, 'I can't stand rows.'

'You just stopped going out with her, is that right?'

'Yes.'

The inspector nibbled one end of his ball-point and stared at his papers. Morley was feeling more composed, his heart, which had been racing, calmed down; he relaxed. The inspector seemed half-hearted and unsure of himself.

'Have you ever seen a girl who has been raped and strangled, Mr Tremain?'

The question was like a blow to the stomach and he had, literally, to catch his breath. But he kept control. He had under-rated the inspector, that was all. But he must be very careful how he reacted. Finally he asked, in a flat voice, 'Are you telling me that Alice is dead?'

He saw at once from the inspector's expression that he had said the right thing. The tension noticeably relaxed again.

'We found her this morning.'

His mind raced. 'Had she been ... Had she been raped?'

'Yes.'

A long silence. It was the inspector who drummed his fingers on the table. Morley sat motionless. In the end he said, 'Where did you find her?'

'In the old mine engine-house.'

Morley said nothing for a while. It was important not to say too much but when it seemed that the inspector would never speak, he asked, 'Have you any idea who did it?'

'Not yet.'

The inspector was looking at him thoughtfully. 'You've hurt your face, Mr Tremain.'

'I did that last Wednesday.'

'I know. How did you do it?'

'I fell down.'

'Not in some sort of fight, say a scrap about Alice?'

'A fight? Certainly not!'

'No, you don't look the sort to get into fights. Perhaps your girl-friend did that to you when you told her to push off?'

The inspector's expression was half-humorous, quizzical. Morley's anger flared.

'That's untrue! I've told you . . .'

The inspector held up his hand. 'All right, Mr Tremain, I believe you. Well, I think that's almost all. There's just one more thing. I would like you to tell me everything you did yesterday afternoon. Can you do that?'

'I think so . . .'

'Good. Write it down, every detail you can remember. Take your time over it. The constable here will help you if you want help and I'll be back in half an hour.' He pushed over a pad and a ball-point pen. 'Don't forget to mention anybody you saw, especially anybody you spoke to.' He glanced at his watch. 'God! It's twenty past one. I'm afraid you've missed your canteen lunch at the office.'

'It doesn't matter.'

'See you in half an hour.'

Morley settled down to write. The constable, seated on a chair by the door, watched him. It was like one of his evening-class

46

exams where, on one or two occasions, he had been the only candidate for a particular paper, closeted in a room with the invigilator.

He wrote steadily, he had always been good at essays and he had no difficulty in giving a coherent and detailed account. In half an hour he had finished but the inspector did not return. The constable offered him a cigarette.

'No thanks, I don't smoke but don't let that stop you.'

The constable put his cigarettes away. 'He'd smell it.'

It was half past two when the inspector finally arrived. 'Sorry to keep you. Is this it?'

He read the statement rapidly. 'Good. Quite a turn of style. And you've signed it. Well, that's all for the moment; I've fixed up a car to take you back.'

At the office they seemed to look at him oddly. They had heard on the grapevine that the police had taken him away and the news about Alice had been on the radio at one o'clock. The girls in his office usually treated him with a certain good-humoured contempt but their attitude now was tinged with respect.

When he got home in the evening his mother did not refer to Alice until after she had served his meal and he had toyed with it for a while before pushing it aside.

'I suppose you've heard.'

'They came to the office.'

'The police?'

'Yes.'

There was no more said until she had made a pot of tea and brought it to the table. She stood by his chair and ran a hand through his hair.

'You're not mixed up in this, are you, Morley?'

'Certainly not.'

'You'd tell me if . . .'

'There's nothing to tell.' He spoke with firmness and finality but he was profoundly shaken by his mother's question.

She poured his tea. 'I've put sugar in it, you need something.'

It was one of those seemingly endless June evenings, a quiet sea

47

and a cloudless sky which changed slowly from blue to turquoise and from turquoise to pale green. Tourists were wandering along the quays as usual; they must have known of the murder but it was none of their business, they were out of it.

'They've been going from house to house, asking questions.'

'Did they come here?'

'No.' His mother was knitting, as always. 'They've taken over the old schoolroom as a sort of office.'

The old schoolroom was the nearest thing the village had to a public hall. Thirty years ago it had been the village school, now it was used for parish meetings, whist drives and socials.

Morley tried to read but he could not concentrate. The house seemed so quiet. It must always have been so but he had not noticed before. Every few minutes he caught himself listening. The click of his mother's needles, an occasional anonymous creak. He was aware of the whole house, each individual room, as though he were in it. He had an odd sensation of breathlessness as though he were waiting for some dramatic event and the house seemed to wait with him.

At nine o'clock there was a ring at the side door. Nothing unusual in that, privileged customers often came to the side door after hours for something they had run out of. His mother laid aside her knitting but he forestalled her.

'I'll go.'

'Mr Morley Tremain?' A plain-clothes detective. A warrant card was shown briefly. 'Inspector Martin would like another word with you, sir.'

'Where is he?'

'In the old schoolroom.'

His mother was coming down the stairs.

'I'm just going along to the old schoolroom for a word with the inspector.'

'How long will you be?'

'I'll be back.' The time-honoured formula came naturally to his lips.

At the corner of the street he turned, his mother was standing in the doorway, looking after him. He could tell that she was near to despair. His own feelings were a mixture of fear and relief. At least he would know what was going on.

The old schoolroom was behind the square, reached by a short alley. Paint was flaking off the green walls and the high windows had not been washed in years. A gilded, cardboard crown fastened to one roof tie and the Royal Cypher to another, a string of flags and some coloured lights left up from the Coronation celebrations of a month before.

Now, trestle tables had been set up. A uniformed constable was typing at one table, at another a detective was making entries in a book. Two Post Office engineers were trailing telephone cables along the wall. At the far end of the room Inspector Martin was talking to an older man, a big man with a grey moustache.

Morley was put to sit at one of the trestle tables, Inspector Martin and the big man sat opposite him.

'This is Detective Superintendent Harris.'

Martin did most of the talking but Morley was aware of the superintendent's calm, speculative gaze.

'We have some new evidence, Mr Tremain, and in view of that evidence I am giving you the chance to make a fresh statement.'

Morley felt the blood flooding into his cheeks. 'I don't know what you mean.'

Martin fixed him with an unblinking stare. 'You know very well what I mean. Don't play games, my boy, it's dangerous. You were seen on the cliffs, to the west of the village, at half past four on Sunday afternoon.'

Morley was not told, but the new evidence had been provided by Alfred Short, one of his aunt's boarders. Morley knew him by sight, a middle-aged man with blond curls, thin on top. He was a naturalist and he spent his holiday tramping the countryside with an expensive camera and a pair of binoculars slung round his neck.

Months later, at the trial, Short was called for the prosecution:

Alfred Short, sworn.

Examined by Mr Eden.

'On Sunday 28th June, at approximately four-thirty in the afternoon, I was on the cliffs to the west of the village about a quarter of a mile short of the ruins of the old engine-house.'

'Did you see someone running towards you from the direction of the engine-house?'

'I did.'

'Did you recognize that person?'

'As he came nearer, yes. It was Morley Tremain, the accused.'

'You were a visitor to the village, yet you recognized this man?'

'Yes, I was staying as a paying guest at his uncle's boarding house and I had seen him at the house several times.'

'Did he pass close to you?'

'Yes, within five yards.'

'Did he speak to you or you to him?'

'No.'

'No?'

'He was in a very agitated state and I am certain that he did not see me.'

'You were hiding?'

'No. He was following a rough path through the gorse and I was sitting in a clearing about fifteen feet away.'

'You said that he was agitated, what made you think so?'

'He was very pale and out of breath, he looked scared.'

'Tell the Court what followed.'

'He ran on for another fifty yards or so then he threw himself down and I could no longer see him.'

'Did you try to discover why he was so upset or did you offer to help him?'

'No, it seemed obvious to me that he was not in a condition in which he would wish to be seen by a stranger.'

'Did you tell his relatives what you had seen?'

'No.'

'And you did not tell the police until next evening?'

'No, the following morning I left early and I was out all day. It was not until I returned in the evening that I heard what had happened and realized the possible significance of what I had seen.'

The superintendent's grey eyes regarded him with detachment. The evidence that you were on the cliffs to the west of the 'illage on Sunday afternoon is irrefutable.'

'I'm sorry, I told a lie; I didn't want to be involved.'

'Does that mean that you wish to make a fresh statement?'

'Yes.' His voice came out queerly; he was frightened. He cleared his throat, 'I . . .'

'Let's have it in writing, Mr Tremain.'

Inspector Martin recited the caution which, hitherto, he had only heard in radio plays. He listened but could not apply the words o himself.

Statement by Morley Charles Tremain. Entered as Exhibit 12.

I have been cautioned by Inspector Martin and told that I am not obliged to say anything unless I wish to do so and that anything I say may be taken down in writing and used in evidence.

(Signed) M. C. Tremain.

On the afternoon of the 28th June at approximately 2.30 I set out for a walk along the cliffs to the west of the village in the direction of Black Head. I did not follow the usual cliff path but kept further inland so that I passed the old mine-workings about a mile and a half from the village. I was alone. I did not have any special purpose in mind and I had not arranged to meet anyone.

I reached the valley which runs down to Wicca Cove but I

did not walk down the valley to the cove as it is usually crowded on fine afternoons. I crossed the stream further up the valley and continued along an old path which is rarely used. I remembered walking it as a child and I thought that I would find out if it was still passable. It was overgrown in places but I managed to get through and I continued as far as Chapel Farm which is nearly three miles from the village. I intended to go through the farm-yard and walk back by way of the road but a large Alsatian dog headed me off and, though I tried several times, I had to give up and turn back the way I had come.

I walked back as far as the ruined engine-house without meeting anyone but, from time to time, I could see people walking along the cliff path below me. I cannot say whether or not they saw me.

When I reached the engine-house I walked round the back and looked inside where there is a square of grass almost completely enclosed by the ruin. I do not know what made me do this. On the grass, behind a mound of rubble, I saw the body of Alice Weekes. She was partly undressed and she lay on her back with her legs apart. Her face was distorted and discoloured. I was frightened and I think I ran away. I did not make any attempt to discover whether she was still alive. I did not report what I had found to the police as I thought that by doing so I should place myself under suspicion.

This statement cancels my earlier statement in which I said that I had walked to the east of the village in the direction of Drum Point.

I have read over this statement and declare it to be true.

(Signed) M. C. Tremain

29th June 1953

It was dark outside and the lamp bulbs in the hall cast a sickly, yellow light. The superintendent had gone, so had the detective and the uniformed constable. Inspector Martin lit a cigarette and puffed smoke upwards to the high cross-beams that were hidden in shadow.

'I am taking you to the divisional police station, Mr Tremain, where you will have the chance to get some rest. Your mother has been told.'

'Am I under arrest?'

'You are helping us with our enquiries.'

'Don't you believe what I told you?'

Martin came and perched himself on the corner of the table at which Morley was sitting.

'You admit to having made one false statement. If you want my advice you will think carefully whether you have now told the whole truth. I'm telling you this for your own good.'

Chapter Four

HE WAS GIVEN a meal, fried sausages with mashed potatoes and peas. To his surprise he ate greedily and afterwards they gave him a jam doughnut and a mug of sweet, strong tea. His cell was small, with a brick wall painted white, a tiny window high up and an inadequate lamp in the middle of the ceiling. He had his own pyjamas and toothbrush so somebody must have collected them. He wondered, without much concern, what they had told his mother.

An elderly sergeant took him to his cell, showed him the toilet and explained the rules like an automaton. He felt impelled to prolong even this human contact and forced himself to ask a question.

'Should I ask for a solicitor?'

The sergeant was curt. 'You're entitled to one.' He was out in the passage already.

'But if you were in my place?'

The ghost of a smile. 'It depends. If you've done nothing wrong and you tell the truth, you don't need a solicitor.'

The light had been switched off and he was lying on his bed, staring at the ceiling. A light from outside, probably a street lamp, was reflected on the ceiling and every now and then a car swished by on a road not far away. He still could not work out exactly where he was in relation to the roads he knew.

For the first time in his life he was locked in. They had taken his wristwatch and he had lost all sense of the passage of time. His thoughts went in circles. If you have done nothing . . . If you tell the truth . . .

'I walked to Drum Point and back.' He had put that into his statement and they had proved him a liar. Somebody had seen

54

him coming away from the place where Alice's body had been found. For him, lying in the face of an accusation was almost a reflex response and yet he was usually believed. 'There's one thing, I can always depend on Morley's word; he never lies to me.' His mother's boast when he was a boy at school. Even his teachers believed him to be truthful. His respect for rules meant that he was seldom in trouble and when he was, his serious manner and his worried expression helped to convince them of his sincerity.

Not this time. And if he told the truth now . . .

His mother always enjoyed the trial reports of a good murder. In the recent Christie trial she had nominated herself judge and jury. 'A man like that, free to mix with ordinary, decent folks! The sooner they hang him the better.' And that very Friday, when the papers carried banner headlines announcing the verdict she purred like a contented cat.

And she had once said of Cedric, 'That boy is on the road to the gallows; you mark my words!' Ironic.

The remarkable thing was that he felt so calm. *He* was not on the road to the gallows. At some point, sooner rather than later, they would let him go. They had nothing against him except that he had lied. Nothing.

He fell asleep and dreamt that his hand was resting on Alice's warm arm; just above the wrist. Her skin was like silk and his hand moved very slowly and gently up her arm; he felt the crease at her elbow and the swelling muscles of her upper arm. He was nearing the arm-pit, aware of the moist, intimate warmth near her breast. He woke and cried hot tears of self-pity. It was a long time before he could get to sleep again and when he woke a second time a constable had brought his breakfast.

He had a solicitor after all, his mother had arranged it and when they asked him, he agreed. Mr Rowse, a plump, bald man who looked as though every visible part of him had been scrubbed and polished until it shone. His glasses had round lenses with the thinnest of gold rims. He sat in the grim little interview room looking benign and he seemed to be on good terms with the inspector.

'If you have nothing serious to hide, Morley, it is a very great mistake to lie. The police are good at finding the truth, they are very thorough.' He had said that when they were alone; now the solicitor was sitting in on a further interrogation by Inspector Martin.

'Did you see Alice Weekes on Sunday afternoon at any time before you found her body?'

'No.'

'You are quite sure?'

'Yes.'

'Were you ever intimate with her?'

'No.'

'Did you ever try to be intimate with her?'

'No.'

'Were you intimate with any other girl?'

'No.'

'Never?'

'Never.'

The blue eyes of the inspector lingered on his face as though willing the truth from him.

'Yet Mr Paul, who runs the chemist's shop in the village, says that on Saturday afternoon you came into his shop and purchased a packet of contraceptives.'

It was unfair, he flushed with anger as well as humiliation. He had stood, watching the shop as unobtrusively as possible, until there were no other customers and Paul was alone behind the counter, then he had gone in. But in the moment it took to cross the road and enter the shop Paul had been joined by his girl assistant and he had had to face the two of them. He had stammered something and she had taken the hint and disappeared into the back room but Paul had made a great parade of asking, 'With or without?' He had vowed that he would never repeat the experience.

'Mr Tremain, did you or did you not, buy a packet of contraceptives on Saturday afternoon?'

'Yes.'

'A packet of three?'

'Yes.'

Inspector Martin ran a hand through his fair curls. 'In the pocket of the blazer you were wearing on Sunday afternoon a constable found a packet containing two contraceptives; what happened to the third?'

'No!'

The inspector looked surprised. 'I don't understand you.'

'I mean that I shan't tell you. I refuse to say anything more.' He looked at Rowse. 'I demand to be allowed to go. I want to go home.'

It was his uncle's evidence which nailed yet another of his lies and finally decided the police to charge him. At the trial Harry was required to give evidence for the prosecution:

Henry John Rule Tremain, sworn.

Examined by Mr Eden.

'You are the prisoner's uncle?'

'Yes, sir.'

'On Sunday 28th June, at approximately 2.30 p.m. were you in one of the bedrooms of your house?'

'I was.'

'What were you doing there?'

'I was cleaning my binoculars.'

'In the bedroom?'

'When I'm not using them I keep them on the chest-of-drawers.'

'After you had cleaned them did you try them out?'

'I did.'

'Tell the Court what you did and what you saw.'

'I was at the window, focusing my glasses on objects at different distances when I noticed people on the top path.'

'Is that unusual?'

'Not unusual exactly but the path isn't used much and it's overgrown in places.'

'How far is the path from your house?'

'About a quarter of a mile as a crow flies.'

'Did you focus your binoculars on these people?'

'I did.'

'Did you recognize them?'

'I saw that one of them was my nephew and the other was Alice Weekes.'

'The prisoner and the murdered girl?'

'Yes, sir.'

'Were they walking towards the village or away from it?'

'Away from the village.'

'In the direction of the old mine-workings?'

'In that direction, yes, sir.'

'Were you surprised to see your nephew with Alice Weekes?'

'Yes, I was.'

'Why?'

'Because I thought that was all over.'

'You thought that they had stopped going out together?'

'Yes.'

'Did you mention what you had seen to any member of your family or to anyone else?'

'Yes, I did. When I went downstairs I said to my wife that I had seen Morley on the top path with Alice Weekes.'

'Was anyone else there when you told your wife you had seen them?'

'My daughter, Eunice, my son, Cedric, and my grandfather. My grandfather is ninety-eight and would not have heard me or wouldn't have understood if he had.'

'When you heard about the murder did you tell the police immediately about what you had seen?'

'No, I did not.'

'Why not?'

'Well, he is my nephew.'

'But later, when you were questioned by the police, you changed your mind?'

'I don't know about changing my mind, sir, I felt that I couldn't keep quiet any longer.'

When he had been charged, he asked Inspector Martin if he should make another statement but Martin discouraged him.

'You have been charged, there is no necessity for you to make another statement at this stage and you would be ill-advised to do so without consulting your solicitor. Mr Rowse will be here later this afternoon, talk to him about it.'

It was Tuesday afternoon, he had been at the police station, helping with enquiries, for seventeen hours and already he seemed to have entered upon a new way of life. Since he had been charged the inspector's manner towards him was certainly not hostile, more proprietorial.

'How much longer shall I be kept here?'

'You will come before the magistrates in the morning, at a special Court.'

'And then?'

'Almost certainly you will be remanded in custody.'

'Here?'

'No, we can't keep you here; prisoners on remand are sent to Exeter.'

That afternoon and evening Mr Rowse spent a great deal of time with him. At the start the solicitor was very cheerful, almost boisterous.

'We are trying to brief Mr Enderby, one of the best defence lawyers in the country. If we get him—'

Morley had resolved to tell the whole truth, 'to make a clean breast of it' as his mother would have said. But already he was confused about some of the details and he was finding it difficult to distinguish between what had actually happened and what he had said in his statements.

Mr Rowse listened attentively while he described how he had

come upon Alice with his cousin and how Cedric had spoken of it the following day.

'And on the strength of that you stopped seeing the girl?'

'Yes.'

'In your statement you said that you had heard about her promiscuity from your uncle.'

'My uncle did say something of the sort but it was actually seeing them together—'

'That was on Wednesday evening?'

'Yes.'

'Did you meet her at all between Wednesday evening and Sunday?'

'Except in the shop, no.'

'Had you arranged the meeting on Sunday?'

'No!'

'Yet on Saturday afternoon you purchased contraceptives.'

'That was nothing to do with Alice.'

Mr Rowse's smooth features wrinkled in concern. 'There was another girl?'

'My cousin, Eunice, I went out with her on Saturday evening.' He knew that he was creating a bad impression but he could not explain. He added, 'I needed someone to—'

'Are you saying that you went out with your cousin on the re-bound?'

'Yes, I suppose that is what it was. I took her to the carnival on Saturday evening.'

The solicitor frowned. 'You told the inspector that you have never had intercourse, was that true?'

'Yes.'

'Then isn't it odd that, going out with your cousin for the first time, you thought it necessary to provide yourself with contraceptives? Is she that sort of girl?'

'Yes—no! I thought you were supposed to help me.'

'I am asking you questions now which the prosecution will be bound to ask later.'

How could he explain? If he tried, how could anyone understand? Would this solicitor, middle-aged, smooth and prosperous, understand that he had tried to take a leaf out of Cedric's book? Could he explain about having a white-collar job? About the Kelvin, the big crusher which had to be repaired overnight and the dirt under Cedric's fingernails? About the blazer with brass buttons? About his overwhelming need to—

'Did you have intercourse with your cousin?'

'No!'

'Then—'

'I tried to.'

'But she wouldn't let you, is that it?'

'No, she wanted me to but I couldn't.' He could hold back no longer, he burst into tears.

Eunice had her say at the trial. She stood in the witness-box wearing a beaver-brown, autumn coat, bought specially for the occasion. She looked deathly pale and she spoke in a low, tense voice. Once the judge asked her to 'speak up'. She had the sympathy of the Court. Dressed in her Sunday-best, the jurors could imagine her singing a solo part in the chapel choir looking just as she did in the witness-box.

Eunice Clara Tremain, sworn.

Examined by Mr Eden.

'On Saturday June 27th, did the accused take you to see the carnival?'

'We went to the carnival together.'

'And after you had seen the carnival, did you go for a walk?'

'Yes.'

'Where did you go and what happened? Tell the Court in your own words.'

'We walked up the hill, out of the village, and turned off

along Treskerry Lane. Some way along there was a gate open and we went into a field—'

'You went into a field. What happened? You went into a field like any pair of lovers might do, there is nothing to be ashamed of in that.'

'We sat down on the hay in a sort of open barn and we talked.'

'You talked; did you make love?'

'No.'

'You merely talked?'

'Well, Morley tried to make love to me but I wouldn't let him.'

'In his attempt to make love to you did the accused use a contraceptive?'

'I'm not sure.'

'You know what a contraceptive is?'

'Yes, but I'm not sure if he used one.'

'Did he become violent?'

'Violent?'

'When you refused to let him have his way, did he attempt to force you?'

'Not force me, no.'

'A very personal question which I must ask you, Miss Tremain, are you a virgin?'

'Yes.'

But in the little buff-walled interview room they were still many weeks from the trial.

Mr Rowse took off his flimsy spectacles and polished them with a spotlessly white handkerchief. He looked at Morley, squint-eyed, 'Now let's come to the Sunday afternoon. On that afternoon you decided to go for a walk alone, is that right?'

'Yes.'

'But you met Alice. Where?'

'On what they call the top path. The path which leads past the old mine-working. She was waiting for me.'

'Waiting for you? How did she know you would be there?'

'I suppose it was because I always do the same thing. When I'm alone I almost always walk that way.'

'Tell me about your meeting.'

Morley held his knees, gripping them with his fingers. How could he tell this man anything about what had happened that afternoon?

He had been walking, striding along mindlessly, paying as little attention to his surroundings as if he had been in a suburban street. In fact, he had been brooding on Eunice; he could not get the image of her pathetic, naked body out of his mind. Suddenly, he was aware of a movement and there she was, sitting on the grass, looking up at him, her lips parted—'Alice!'

'I don't think I said anything. We just walked along and she talked. She tried to explain how it had come about with her and Cedric and she told me how she had got into bad company when they lived in Redruth.

'She said that she wanted to make a fresh start, that she really loved me and that what had happened with Cedric would never happen with anybody again.'

'Did you believe her?'

'I don't know. I wanted to.'

Looking back the whole incident had about it an inevitability which he did not understand. It was as though he had been following a script written for him by somebody else. The scene had been set for reconciliation and that was what he had wanted but, perversely, he had said the wrong words, harsh and bitter words. He did not realize even now that his mother, his aunt, his uncle and, even Cedric, had been speaking for him.

'What did she say?'

He was staring at the table-top and he did not look up. 'She didn't say anything, she just looked at me then she turned back the way we came and left me standing there. I think that she was crying.'

'What did you do?'

He put his hand to his forehead as though he had a headache.

'I wanted to call after her but I didn't, I don't know why. I watched her walking away from me and then I continued on the way I was going.'

'What did you do?'

'I did what I said in my statement, I walked along the old path as far as Chapel Farm where I intended to get on to the road but the dog stopped me.'

'And on your way back you found her?'

He nodded.

It must have been a very warm afternoon, the sun was striking on the frosted glass of the little interview room and, from time to time, the solicitor mopped his forehead with a handkerchief. There were little beads of perspiration under his eyes.

'Now think, Morley: where were you when Alice turned back, on the village side of the mine-workings or beyond them?'

'Beyond them by a good quarter of a mile.'

'One more question. On your walk, going or coming, did you see anyone you knew?'

'No, no one.'

'You are sure?'

'Yes—wait a minute! I never thought of it before, I've just remembered. From the old engine-house, as you are coming along the top path you can see the slope of the hill down to my uncle's house and I saw Cedric going down the hill to his house.'

'It must be a considerable distance from the old engine-house; are you sure it was your cousin?'

'Quite sure. I couldn't mistake Cedric, in any case he was clear against the sky, he stood out.'

'Was he hurrying—walking or running?'

'The slope is so steep there you haven't much choice, you slide a certain amount whatever you do.'

Cedric, too, was called by the prosecution. He was in Court only briefly and he never glanced at the dock. He looked pale and he seemed to have lost weight.

Cedric Themain, sworn.

Examined by Mr Eden.

'Do you remember Sunday 28th June?'

'Yes, sir, I do.'

'What were you doing on that afternoon?'

'After lunch on that day I had an upset stomach and I went to bed.'

'What time did you have lunch?'

'The usual time for lunch on a Sunday, sir, about half past one.'

'Did you get up at all that afternoon or evening?'

'Except to go to the toilet, no, sir.'

Throughout the trial, which lasted three days, Morley sat in the dock but he found it difficult to believe, to really believe, that the slow, archaic procedures had anything to do with him. Counsel, and even the judge, made foolish little jokes from time to time and the Court laughed. Most of the time nobody paid any attention to him.

'How do you plead, guilty or not guilty?'

'Not guilty.'

His voice had sounded cracked and, foolishly, he wanted to say the words again, more convincingly, but he did not get the chance.

There were two women on the jury; one of them was very fat and jolly looking. Once, he could have sworn, she winked at him. The other . . . The other woman reminded him of his mother. He could almost hear her saying, 'There's no smoke without fire. They don't get this far if they aren't guilty. The police know what they're doing.'

During the medical evidence about the condition of Alice's body he was aware of her eyes on him, little black eyes. Thumbs down every time.

They had succeeded in persuading his mother not to come.

It was when they took him back to his cell each night that the really bad times came. He had books, old favourites, and he read himself to sleep. *Kidnapped, Catriona, The Courts of the Morning* . . .

'How much longer will it go on?'

'It will be over tomorrow.'

'Can I appeal?'

'You haven't been convicted yet.'

Extract from the Closing Speech for the Prosecution.

Mr Eden: The defence maintains that the encounter between the accused and the dead girl on Sunday 28th June, was accidental, that they had not arranged to meet in advance. You will come to your own conclusion about that but you may be influenced by the fact that the accused had contraceptives in the pocket of the jacket he was wearing. Furthermore it has been established in evidence that this was not the jacket he wore the previous evening when he was out with his cousin, Eunice Tremain. At that time he was wearing a blazer. You have also heard in evidence that he transferred the packet of contraceptives to his other jacket so that his mother would not find them while he was out. You may think this an implausible explanation. The accused is not a boy of sixteen but a man of twenty-two and it is unlikely that he would feel accountable to his mother for his conduct in such matters.

I suggest to you that, stimulated by what he had heard and seen of this girl, whom he had previously believed to be chaste, he decided to behave towards her in the way others had done. If that were all we should not be here today and the prisoner would not be in the dock. You have heard the medical evidence and you will, no doubt, accept that Alice Weekes died while resisting an attempt at rape. You may think this an ironic and improbable fate for a girl with her reputation but the medical evidence has not been contested by the defence. Indeed, I venture to say that it is incontestable. That evidence also asserts

66

that Alice Weekes must have died shortly before the time at which the accused was seen running away from the engine-house where her body was found. I see from a transcript of the evidence that Dr Ashby, the pathologist, when asked what he meant by 'shortly' replied that he could not be more precise so, ladies and gentlemen of the jury, it is left to you to put your own interpretation on his words . . .

. . . I come now to the assertion by the accused in one of his several statements to the effect that he saw his cousin Cedric Tremain running down the slope to his house. I am sure that the implication of this convenient recollection did not escape you. The prosecution does not have to answer random, unsupported statements of this kind but, nevertheless, you will have noted also that it was the unanimous statement of Cedric Tremain's mother, father and sister, that he did not leave the house that afternoon. He was, in fact, confined to his bed with a severe bilious attack brought on by something he had eaten . . .

Extract from Mr Justice Burton's Charge to the Jury.

. . . Members of the jury, I have done my best to assist you in your task. Your responsibility is a grave one. You have in your hands the whole future of this young man, but you must not let your awareness of that responsibility deter you from arriving at a true verdict. It is a common misconception that a jury must have incontrovertible proof before they may properly convict. That is not so. If you are satisfied in your minds beyond reasonable doubt that the prisoner is guilty as charged then you must so declare. To find the prisoner guilty as charged you must be satisfied beyond reasonable doubt that, first, it was he who accomplished the death of Alice Weekes and, second, that in pursuing the course of action which led to her death he realized that death or serious injury might result. If you are in genuine doubt on either of these counts then you must give the prisoner the benefit of that doubt and acquit him.

Members of the jury, will you consider your verdict.

(The jury retired at 3.58 p.m. and returned into Court at 5.30 p.m.)

The Clerk of Court: Members of the jury, are you agreed upon your verdict?

The Foreman of the Jury: We are.

The Clerk of the Court: Do you find the prisoner at the Bar, Morley Charles Tremain, guilty or not guilty?

The Foreman of the Jury: We find him guilty.

The Clerk of the Court: You find him guilty, and that is the verdict of you all?

The Foreman of the Jury: It is the verdict of us all.

The Clerk of Court: Prisoner at the Bar, you stand convicted of murder; have you anything to say before judgement of death is passed according to law?

The Prisoner at the Bar: I am not guilty, I did not kill her!

The Judge: Morley Charles Tremain, you have been found guilty of a terrible crime. The sentence of the Court upon you is that you be taken from this place to a lawful prison and thence to a place of execution, and that you be there hanged by the neck until you be dead; and that your body be afterwards buried within the precincts of the prison in which you shall be confined before your execution. And may the Lord have mercy on your soul.

PART TWO

1974

Chapter Five

SIX O'CLOCK ON a June morning; a misty start to the day, a pearly opalescence which would soon disperse before the sun. Harry Tremain, now sixty-five, spare and still fit, walked along the quay to where his dinghy was moored by the steps. He carried a small basket of bait. He was officially retired but he kept a few crab-pots mainly as an excuse to have a boat on the water. *Green Lady III* had been sold and, with a blue hull, she was now working out of Falmouth. Her successor, *Green Lady IV*, lay at her moorings in the inner harbour. She was a smaller boat, a launch with a decked-in fo'c's'le and a wooden and glass screen to shelter the helmsman. The single engine in the well was protected by a wooden housing with a sloping top like a dog kennel, but her hull was painted pea-green like her predecessors.

Harry sculled out to her and climbed aboard. He started the motor, transferred the mooring buoy to the punt, knocked in the motor and glided across the inner harbour. He stood with one hand resting lightly on the little wheel. The time of day he liked best, the only time when he seemed to be truly himself.

Across the outer harbour, weaving between the moorings. He could almost have done it with his eyes closed. Fifty-one years ago he had left school and started fishing full time with his grandfather in *Green Lady III*. His grandfather had been about the same age then as he was now yet he had seemed to the young Harry a really old man. He scarcely remembered his father, blown up in a minesweeper during the first war.

He felt the bows lift to the swell as he came through the pier-heads out into the bay.

A pity that Cedric had not carried on the family tradition which had been unbroken for at least a hundred and seventy years. Cedric

71

was now in his forties, married with a daughter of twenty but living separated from his wife. Seven years ago Cedric had lost his job at the quarry for being too free with his fists and Harry had allowed himself to be persuaded to buy the local garage, which happened to be on the market, and to set Cedric up there. The garage was prosperous, it could hardly fail to be with no other in the village, but Cedric was always in debt, he drank a great deal more than was good for him and he was dishonest.

The mist was parting, opening a path of silky blue-green water ahead. Looking back it was clear enough to see the village, no longer a neat pyramid but a sprawl of houses spread out like a hand clutching at the hillside. Now he was beginning to feel the growing warmth of the sun through his jersey.

His first pot was fairly close under the cliffs to the west of the breakwater so he headed inshore. He knocked out the motor and glided alongside the string of floating corks, deftly fishing them aboard with a boat-hook. He hauled away at the line and brought up the pot which was empty though the bait had gone.

He still lived in the slate-fronted house on the quay but his wife, Clara, was dead and he shared the house with Eunice, her husband and child. Eunice had married a laboratory assistant from the technical college and they had a child, a boy of four who was spoiled and seemed to spend his time whining at his mother. Eunice was stringier than ever and her tongue had become sharper with the years. She was mean too, cheeseparing.

He could take little pleasure in his children.

He baited the pot and lowered it back. Under the cliffs the water seemed dark but very clear and he thought he could glimpse a vague outline of the pot on the bottom. He threw the corks overboard, knocked in the motor and went back to the wheel. He cruised along the coast as far as the entrance to Wicca Cove. Even at this hour there were two people on the beach, a boy and a girl. The girl had her arms upraised, doing something with her hair, her young body outlined against the white sand. A surge of desire took him by surprise and was followed by a wave of sadness. His next pot produced a crab.

He made his rounds then stood off a little before taking the broad sweep that would bring him round the breakwater and into harbour. Off Wicca Cove he left the wheel, picked up some cotton waste and went to the engine housing. He lifted the starboard flap and glimpsed momentarily the little engine with its rusty exhaust pipe, the last thing he would ever see. A tremendous blast of hot air and an explosion he did not hear, though it set all the gulls along that part of the coast squawking and screaming. His body was lifted clean out of the boat, it described a broad arc in the air, seemed to levitate for a brief moment, then fell like a rag doll into the sea. *Green Lady IV*, holed below the water line, settled slowly, her motor still running until water reached the carburettor. A couple of crab-pots, the bait basket, a boat-hook, a pair of sweeps and splintered fragments of the engine house floated free before she finally submerged and sank.

It happened that the launch had been off Wicca Cove when she blew up and the young couple had seen it all. They stood, side by side on the beach, spellbound, until the launch finally disappeared and they were the only witnesses. The girl, a pretty brunette, who had unwittingly given Harry Tremain his last tremor of sexual excitement, described what they had seen.

'We saw the launch pass the mouth of the cove close in, then about half-an-hour later she came back, further out to sea but still close enough for us to see the man at the wheel. While we were watching he left the wheel and seemed to be bending over the engine and a few seconds later the explosion came. Bits shot up into the air and the man too. It was just like a film, you couldn't believe it was real. We just stood and watched the boat sink. The funny thing was the bang didn't seem very loud, I mean, you get a much louder bang from the quarries when they're blasting. At first it didn't occur to us that we ought to do anything, I suppose we were shocked, but then I said to Mick, "Well, what if nobody else saw it?" Anyway we got up to the farm on the road as soon as we could and they telephoned from there.'

Walter Tyson heard the explosion which sank *Green Lady IV* and killed Harry Tremain. He was an early riser and he liked to

walk round the camping site before his staff arrived. There was a
mist, thin and suffused with light but more than enough to shut
out his view of the great broad expanse of the bay. Even the elm
trees which bordered the site were no more than shadowy shapes
against the sky. In half-an-hour or an hour it would clear and there
would be another glorious day. He looked at his watch, it was a
quarter to seven. Perhaps his heart was beating a little faster than
usual but otherwise he was calm. He stood still a moment, listening. Was it possible that the mist . . . ? He walked on.

The site was full; a hundred and twenty tourist caravans, twelve
residentials and about four hundred and fifty tents. Altogether, say
sixteen hundred men, women and children. Quite a large village
and he was responsible for them. He supplied them with their
bread, milk, newspapers and most of their groceries, their heating
and lighting. Washing facilities, toilets, refuse and sewage disposal
were in his charge and it was also his job to keep order, to see
that the site rules were obeyed. It was a great responsibility and
he was proud to do the job well.

Ten minutes to seven. The vans and tents where there were
young children were always awake first and already people
were converging on the wash-ups, tramping over the wet grass.
He wished that they would keep to the paths. The doors of several
vans were clipped back and he could see women in dressing-gowns
busy preparing breakfasts. Young people were always the last to
stir and some of the tent flaps would remain closed until eleven
or even later.

Five minutes to seven. He was concerned. He stood still, looking
at his watch, at the seconds hand while it swept the circumfer-
ence and almost another. He happened to be near the entrance, not
far from his own caravan. A dull boom and a distant squawking
of gulls which soon died away. He relaxed and walked back to his
caravan.

At half-past seven his staff arrived, three women who served in
the shop, three more who looked after the wash-ups and toilets and
an odd-job man. He unlocked the shop and the implements store,
issued a 'float' for the check-out till and stood watching the trickle

74

of early customers who would get only yesterday's milk and bread because the new deliveries were not due until eight o'clock.

'Did you hear that bang?' He could not resist asking the girl at the check-out.

She looked up at him with indifferent, heavily made-up eyes. 'What?'

'A bang, just before seven.'

'I never hear nothing till I get here, I'm only half awake now.'

'I heard it, just as I was coming out of my front door.' An older woman, busy stacking milk-crates ready for the milkman. 'I thought it was the quarry. Why? Was it something special?'

He shook his head. 'No, I just wondered; they don't usually start blasting at the quarry until twelve o'clock.'

He always went back to his caravan to listen to the weather forecast and the News and to have his breakfast.

'Mist now affecting parts of Devon and Cornwall will soon clear giving another fine, sunny day over the whole region. Temperatures are expected to rise to 21° Centigrade, 70° Fahrenheit on the coasts and higher inland . . .'

He had learned patience.

After his boiled egg with whole-meal bread and two cups of coffee he washed up his dirty dishes then went across to his little office in Reception. He had not been sitting there long when the first 'departure' drew up at the barrier, a Ford Escort towing a box trailer in which a tent was stowed. A man in khaki shorts got out and came to the window leaving his wife and two children in the car.

'Leaving us?'

'Have to, I'm afraid. Got to get back. The name's Browning. We arrived a week ago.'

Tyson leafed through the ledger. 'Here we are, Mr Browning, seven nights, vehicle and tent with four persons. I think you'll find that right, Mr Browning.'

A five-pound note. Change. Good wishes for the journey and the day had really begun.

He liked people who stayed several nights, he got to know them and after the first day or two they no longer avoided looking at him, his appearance no longer embarrassed them.

At half-past nine the postman drove up in his little van and brought the news.

'I suppose you've heard?' Willie Yates, the postman, asked the question though he supposed no such thing.

'Heard what?' He was careful to sound off-hand.

'Old man Tremain's launch blew up when he was out seeing to his pots this morning. The launch went down and there's no sign of Harry, not yet, anyway.'

Tyson's heart beat faster but he gave no sign of more than ordinary concern. 'Blew up? What happened?'

'Nobody knows, it's a mystery. They talked about him striking a mine but if he had there would have been a hell of a blast. Now they're saying it must have been a petrol leak.'

Willie pushed the bundle of mail through the window.

'Lucky you wasn't out with the old man this morning.'

Occasionally he went out with Harry Tremain when he was seeing to his pots but not, as now, at the height of the season.

He managed to say, casually, 'Not much chance of that, this time of year.'

He spent most of the morning in Reception with occasional sallies to see how things were going in the shop and round the site. At ten thirty a girl brought him a cup of coffee and two rich-tea biscuits, at twelve he shut the window and placed a notice by it: 'Reception closed until 2 p.m.'

Then he walked down the hill to the village and along the waterfront to the public bar of the Robartes Arms. In contrast with the saloon, which was crowded with tourists, there were few customers in the public bar. Two men in peaked caps and blue jerseys played dominoes, looking like a Celtic version of Cézanne's Card Players. Three or four others looked on. They acknowledged Walter with friendly nods or a muttered word and he went to the bar for his drink.

His acceptance in the public bar had meant a lot to him. When he had come to the village two years earlier it had been the strangest experience of his life, like coming back from the dead and not being recognized. Although he had sought that very situation he had suffered; for a while he seemed to have no identity, not even a name, for when they spoke of him they called him, simply, 'the man with no face'. Now he was Walter and nobody looked at him a second time.

'Willie Yates told me about Harry Tremain.'

Conversation in the bar was always punctuated by long silences and he was not concerned at the absence of an immediate reply.

'A funny ol' business,' from one of the domino players.

There was a discussion about pleasure craft which had blown up as a result of accidents with bottled gas but nobody could suppose that Harry Tremain had any such thing aboard.

'I suppose they'll have an inquest.'

'Bound to, but they got to find him first.'

The low-ceilinged room was dimly lit and cool like a cave but the door stood open to the quay, a blinding rectangle of light. A big man with an enormous paunch came in and went to the counter. Instead of a cap and jersey he wore a suit, it had been a good suit at one time but now it was heavily stained with oil and grease.

'The usual, Jacko.'

While he waited to be served he turned to face the company who acknowledged him as they had done Walter. The barman served him a double then somebody said, 'We was very sorry to hear about your father, Ceddie, very sorry.'

There was a general murmur of assent.

He lit a cigarette with unsteady hands. 'I know, I know.' Although his features were florid there were ugly livid patches under his eyes. No insurance doctor would have looked at him twice.

'Any idea what happened?'

'Not a clue.' He smoked nervously then seemed to think that more was required of him. 'The old man could never leave well alone, he was always tinkering. I reckon he got a petrol leak which flashed from the electrics or maybe from the exhaust.'

One of the players, a thin man, horse-faced and shrewd, said, 'He'd have been on paraffin surely?'

'Should have been. Should have been, of course. But half the time he'd forget to switch over; always getting the bloody plugs sooted up.'

The thin man placed a double blank in position and looked to see his opponent's reaction before turning again to Cedric.

'I saw you go off to the launch yesterday afternoon and I thought then he must be having trouble.'

'Timing, that's all that was. He'd been buggering about with the timing and it was all to hell. He asked me to take a look so as he could go out this morning.'

Cedric placed his glass on the counter and signed to the barman for a refill. His movements were slow and uncertain but he was making an effort to appear composed.

The other domino player, a stocky little man with skin like polished mahogany, spoke for the first time.

'They haven't found him yet?'

'Not yet. You know how it is; tide on the ebb. I reckon he'll fetch up down the coast in the course of a tide or two.'

Walter sat sipping his beer without saying a word. It was incredible. He had never imagined that it would be like this; everybody seemed to accept the fact that a man had been blown up while going about his daily business as though it were a common occurrence. What had he expected? More drama, tension; certainly a greater concern. In a way, he felt cheated. Yet things were going to plan. But it was essential that the body should be found. What would the authorities do if it wasn't? He did not know. Would they try to raise the launch? Either way it was just possible that an inquest would decide that Harry Tremain had met his death through an accident though the accident could not be explained. Death from misadventure? That would be the final irony and he put the idea from his mind. He was surprised that no one seemed to have linked the explosion with the theft of explosives from the quarry a month earlier.

Coastguards and men from the village searched for the body without success and their efforts were hindered by almost continuous rain. But two days after the explosion, on the Wednesday, the body was found by holiday makers, three miles down the coast, wedged in a gully. It was taken to the mortuary of the pathology department at the county hospital and examined by Dr Franks who reported to the coroner. Certain fragments of metal embedded in the tissues bothered the pathologist.

The coroner was incredulous. 'You're not suggesting a bomb? Who would want to blow up an old fellow——?'

Franks, who did not like the coroner, was curt, 'I'm not suggesting anything, I'm telling you what I found.'

There was plenty of gossip but nobody in the village had much to go on. The coroner opened an inquest on Thursday afternoon and after taking evidence of finding and identification, adjourned. Walter Tyson went about his work as usual and if he was under any strain he did not show it.

At the ironmonger's, where he bought odds and ends for minor repairs at the site, the proprietor was lugubriously philosophic but he summed up the general feeling in the village.

'You never know what's in store for you, Mr Tyson; that's what I always say. Poor old Harry! Well, there's some I could name as won't shed no tears. Come as a blessing I shouldn't wonder.' He paused to let his point sink home then continued. 'They're a funny family, the Tremains. Of course, you wouldn't remember Sidney. Harry's brother. He hanged himself in Harry's fish loft—just like that! No reason, seemingly. Must've been queer in the head but you'd never think so—quiet sort of chap. Then there was Sidney's son . . .'

Tyson did not hear about the son because a customer, a stranger, came in and the ironmonger had to turn his attention to business. But as he was leaving the shop his disfigured features were twisted into what might have been a smile.

On Friday the fine weather returned and when Willie Yates brought the post he had more news.

'They've called the Navy in.'

He knew at once what was meant but he asked vaguely, 'The Navy?'

'Salvage team from the dockyard.'

'Who's paying for that—Cedric?'

'Not likely. From what I hear it's the authorities who aren't satisfied. It seems they've been over the cove since first light. If it's all gone right they'll have the hawsers under her by now and she'll be lifting when the tide begins to flow. They'll bring her in on the flood.'

Every villager understood the sea, you didn't have to be one of the cap and jersey brigade.

Walter risked a question. 'What do they think, then?'

Willie shook his head. 'I've no idea but I've heard talk that they've been down to the quarry about the jelly that was nicked a few weeks back.' He chuckled. 'Anyway, I don't think they're getting her up for Cedric's benefit.'

His patience was being rewarded, it proved that all he had to do was to sit and wait.

Green Lady IV came up without difficulty. At low water it was easy for the naval skin-divers to sling hawsers under her keel and these were secured to floats on the surface. As the tide turned she lifted clear and on the top of the flood they towed her into the inner harbour. When Walter went for his mid-day drink she was lying on the bottom, her stumpy mast just clearing the surface of the water. It gave him an odd feeling to join the crowd of tourists who stood on the quay staring down into the green water as though they expected something to happen.

He was there again at six o'clock when the tide had left her and there she was, listing to starboard but looking much as usual except for a gaping hole in her planks, jagged, roughly oval, and about two feet in diameter. Oily water trickled out of her causing a patch of iridescence in the black mud of the harbour bed. People lined the quays and there was almost a holiday atmosphere like the evening of regatta day when everyone comes to watch the water sports. A powerful tractor with a winch was warming up on the wharf at the top of the slipway and men in thigh boots were laying skids and rollers.

The operation was being directed by the harbour master but he seemed to defer to a dapper gentleman in a light grey suit who, the bystanders said, was a detective.

Cedric was standing at the top of the slipway with his sister, Eunice. Her thin, bony figure, utterly devoid of feminine charm, her pale face and bulging forehead combined to make her as unattractive in her own way as Cedric was in his. They were not part of the crowd; the spectators, recognizing their special interest, stood back and left them alone. Cedric had offered his help with getting the launch up the slipway and he had been refused by the harbour master.

'What the hell do they think they're doing? After all, she's mine now.'

'You hope.'

Cedric looked at his sister, his anger tempered by vague misgiving. 'What's that supposed to mean?'

'There's no will found yet but I know he made one and so do you.'

'So?'

The pale skin which stretched over her forehead wrinkled into a frown. 'Just this, Cedric, you've been sponging on father since you left school and you've never done a hand's turn for him. Don't forget that he's been living with me since mother died and it's me that's had to do for him. If he felt that you'd had your share— and more than your share already—you'd have no cause to complain.' She spoke in a sibilant whisper so that no word of what she said reached the bystanders.

Cedric's colour heightened. 'Living with you? I like that! I bloody well like that! You and that precious husband of yours moved in on the old man lock, stock and bloody barrel before mother was in her grave and you've been living there on the cheap ever since.' He paused in an attempt to control his anger. 'If it comes to that—'

'Keep your voice down unless you want the whole village to hear.'

He was about to make an explosive reply but, abruptly, changed his mind. 'Oh, well, there's no point in arguing. There's a will all right—or there was.'

Eunice's voice was quietly menacing. 'What do you mean by that? Are you suggesting that I destroyed his will?'

He did not really believe any such thing but he was sullen like a bad-tempered child. 'I don't know, do I?'

Two little spots of colour appeared on her sallow cheeks. 'Just think of this, Cedric. If there is no will you'll get a half share, but if there is you might very well get damn all—which is what you deserve. And another thing, before you start any malicious talk about me just think of your own position and ask yourself *why* they're salvaging the launch. Do you think it's for your benefit?'

He was scared. It was as though a great ravine had suddenly opened at his feet. For years he had been saying to himself, over and over again, 'When the old man goes—. When the old man goes—.' Now he was gone and the bare possibility that he had left his money elsewhere made Cedric come out in a cold sweat. He had always assumed that Eunice would get the house and a thousand or two but anything more was unthinkable. And what did she mean about them salvaging the launch? Was she hinting—? He looked at his sister and felt slightly reassured. He knew her, she loved to put the boot in; looking as she did it was the only thrill she could expect. She was a bitch but he didn't seriously think that she would have destroyed the old man's will. And there was a will, his father had told him that much often enough. As to the other—well, that was just Eunice, but he would have to be careful, he couldn't afford to get her really needled.

It took a good deal more than an hour to get *Green Lady IV* up the slipway out of reach of the next high tide. The crowd thinned as the time for their evening meal drew near but Eunice and Cedric stood their ground as though each thought the other might gain some unforeseen advantage if left alone.

In fact, as they both knew very well, *Green Lady IV* was among the least of Harry Tremain's assets. In the fifties he had bought several of the old fish lofts, converted them and let them on fifteen-year leases to shops and cafés. The leases fell in when property was at its peak and Harry sold. He had died a rich man.

Tyson was standing not far from them and, although he could not hear what they said, he knew as most of the bystanders knew, that they were bickering. It was rare for brother and sister to be seen together and as he watched them he tried to analyse his feelings. More accurately, he tried to find some spark of emotion which they kindled in him. He had reason enough to hate but he could feel only indifference. If his life had been tragic, theirs had been, and was, pathetic; he almost found it in his heart to pity them.

The inner contradiction puzzled and worried him. He could not begin to explain it. He remembered a book of Simenon's—he was a great reader—called *A New Lease of Life*. The central character had met and overcome a great crisis and afterwards he had consciously and deliberately set out to lead a completely different life. As though he had been born again. Tyson had had two great crises in his life and he had overcome them—at least, he had survived. Surely he was entitled to a new beginning? He had tried and, to some extent, succeeded in making a new life. In more than one sense he was a different person, but a condition of true rebirth is forgetfulness. Well, he wanted to forget but memory clung to him like Sinbad's incubus.

His life in the village and his job at the camping site satisfied him, he was not conscious of frustration or of great bitterness, not even of much self-pity, yet he felt compelled to behave as though he were driven on by hatred in a senseless effort to even some imaginary score. Whenever, as now, he had begun to feel settled, to be at ease with life, his contentment was eroded by a sense of guilt. Guilt! Yes, that was the word. But of what was he guilty —he, who had always been a victim? When he tried to answer that question absurd ideas came into his mind, pictures rather than ideas, images of his childhood and youth—they made no sense.

The detective and a man in overalls were examining the hole in the side of the launch.

'Definitely from the inside, no question about that.'

The launch was supported on an improvised cradle and they had put a short ladder against her side. The detective climbed into her awkwardly and the other followed.

'Surprisingly little damage to the engine except for the sump.'

'Yes, and like I said, the fuel intake is on the other side.'

The men who had helped with the salvage went off to the pub and later the detective and his mechanic drove off leaving a uniformed constable to guard the launch. He stayed all night and was relieved by another in the morning. The villagers were left in no doubt of the view taken by the authorities.

On the Regional News in the morning the news reader said, 'The death of Mr Harry Tremain as a result of an explosion aboard his launch on Monday last is to be further investigated by the police. Detective Chief Inspector James Gill, who has been put in charge, said last night that he was treating it as a case of murder.'

When Tyson went for his lunchtime drink there was a large police trailer-caravan parked on ground opposite where *Green Lady IV* was drawn up on her cradle. A patrol car and two other cars were parked nearby. Tourists and trippers gawped at the launch and at the van but the van windows were fitted with one-way glass so that nothing could be seen of what went on inside. There were plenty of comings and goings, mainly of large men in crumpled lounge suits, obviously detectives. At the pub on the quay Tyson learned that the chief inspector had personally interviewed Eunice and Cedric and that Cedric had been with him for more than an hour.

Harry Tremain's body had been released for burial by the coroner and the funeral took place on Saturday afternoon. Like most village funerals, apart from the hearse, there were no cars. The encoffined body had been brought to the slate house on the quay and at half past two a procession began to form there to walk to the cemetery which was half way up the hill out of the village. Cedric and Eunice walked behind the hearse; Eunice in unrelieved black which, the gossips said, was the same as she had worn at her mother's funeral. Cedric looked ill and from time to time he seemed to stagger so that it was doubtful whether he would make it to the cemetery, but he did. Cedric's daughter walked with her mother who caused a great deal of surprise by being there at all. Behind them, everybody who was anybody, altogether more than two hundred people, followed the coffin. Walter Tyson was there and his companion, Charlie Pullen, the elder of the two domino players, pointed to a stranger, a very tall, thin man with rubbery features.

'That's Gill, the head detective.'

And it was Charlie Pullen who, in the bar that evening, gave Walter the real news of the day. As it was Saturday there were more customers than usual and there were two reporters standing drinks. Charlie spoke quietly, his eye on the reporters.

'Who do you think gets the old man's money, then?'

Walter sipped his beer before replying; an unreflective reply was always considered frivolous.

'Fifty fifty, Cedric and Eunice is my guess.'

'Then you guess wrong.' Charlie paused to make his play in the domino game. 'Eunice gets the house and that's all; not a penny.'

'Then Cedric has done pretty well for himself.'

'You think so?'

'If he gets everything bar the house—'

'He don't. He gets damn all.'

'Then who—?'

'Laura, Cedric's girl, gets the lot.'

Charlie's partner, younger, cheerful and stout, always let his senior fire the big guns but now he joined in, slapping his thigh with enjoyment.

'What do you think of that, then, Walter me boy? What you think of that, then?'

'I can hardly believe it.'

'It's true enough, I had it from Eunice's husband, poor little toad, he's nearly 'bout afraid to go home.'

Walter could imagine Eunice's fury.

'The last I heard they couldn't find a will.'

'Well, they've found one now and I bet they wishes they hadn't.'

The police enquiry continued on Sunday but very little news leaked out to the villagers, so that it was from the radio on Monday morning that they learned of the next major development.

'Cedric Tremain, son of the murdered man, has been at the Divisional Police Station since ten o'clock last night, helping the police with their enquiries.'

Tyson heard the announcement when he listened to the bulletin, as usual, at eight o'clock and a weight lifted from his shoulders.

On the nine o'clock news that evening it was announced that Cedric had been charged with his father's murder and when Walter did his rounds that evening he felt that he was really beginning on a new lease of life.

By Tuesday lunchtime the police trailer had gone from the quay and there was no longer a guard on *Green Lady IV*.

Chapter Six

I T W A S C H A N C E which brought Detective Chief Superintendent Wycliffe to the village; no more than coincidence that he had
chosen to stay at a place which had so recently been the scene of
a murder. He had been ill. A persistent cold had become influenza and influenza had paved the way for pneumonia. Now, after
six weeks, the doctor had ordered a month's recuperative leave.
It had been his first major illness and it had shaken him more
than he would admit. On his last visit to the doctor, while tucking
in his shirt, he had said shyly, 'I suppose I *shall* get back to
normal?'

The doctor had looked at him over his glasses, his thin lips
twitched, 'Oh, I think you can count on a year or two more of
active life.'

He wondered if he was quite as supercilious when people asked
him silly questions in the course of his professional life.

'What do you think I'll get, Mr Wycliffe?'

Or, from the first offender, 'What's it like in prison?'

A parting shot from his doctor: 'Just remember that you're
forty-eight, not twenty-four.'

It happened that his daughter, Ruth, had been invited to spend
part of the summer with the Wordens who had a summer cottage
near the village. Ruth had met the Worden son at university and
now there was a distinct possibility that they would marry. Helen
approved but Wycliffe secretly hoped that it would come to
nothing. Worden senior was a stockbroker and, in Wycliffe's view,
stockbrokers would hardly stand a camel's chance when it came at
last to the needle's eye. In any case the boy was too smooth.

It was Mrs Worden's idea that Wycliffe and Helen should spend
part of their enforced holiday close by so that the two families

could get to know each other. The unspoken thought seemed to be that on neutral ground they could size each other up without commitment. The Wycliffes booked in at an hotel in the village but neutral ground turned out to be a thirty-foot ketch which Worden had hired with a man to crew. For two days, in glorious weather, they had cruised up and down the coast, bathed and fished, picnicked and made forays inland at unlikely spots. It would have been idyllic but for one thing. Ruth spent her time with the boy, Helen and Mrs Worden seemed to take to one another and Wycliffe was left with the stockbroker. He decided that the motion of the boat upset him and Helen, sensible woman, agreed to believe him and was even sympathetic.

'What a pity! Never mind, there are plenty of other things we can do.'

'There's no reason why you shouldn't continue to go out with the Wordens.'

'Oh, I couldn't, not without you.'

'I don't see why not. I shall be happy enough pottering about the village. You know me.'

'You're sure?'

'Of course!'

'They do seem to be very nice people and it is a chance to get to know them better.'

'Just one thing . . . If Ruth does decide to marry that boy—'

'Well?'

He shrugged his shoulders, hardly knowing himself what he wanted to say.

'Don't *worry* so, Charles! Ruth is a sensible girl.'

Next morning there was a heavy mist but the sun broke through before eight o'clock, promising another perfect day. As soon as they had finished breakfast they went down to the quay together, he to see Helen off on yet another cruise. The ketch was moored in the outer harbour but Worden had brought the dinghy into the basin and was sculling round off the steps, waiting. When he caught sight of them his fleshy, lobster-red face lit with pleasure. There could be no doubt that he was a cheerful, friendly man and to his astonishment Wycliffe had found him disarmingly straight-forward and uncomplicated; to be honest, rather stupid.

Helen slid expertly into the dinghy and a minute or two later they had disappeared into the outer harbour. Wycliffe strolled along the waterfront feeling, illogically, disgruntled; a man, for once, with all the time in the world. It happened to be exactly one week since Cedric Tremain had been taken into custody to be charged with his father's murder.

Before eleven in the morning and after six at night the village recaptured something of the charm which it had had before mass tourism became a major commercial racket. There were no cars parked on the quays, the gift shops were closed and the pavements were free of their overspill of junk; there were few people about and those who were took time to look around them. The real shops were doing business, selling bread, meat, milk, fruit and vege-tables; the cap and jersey brigade were pumping out bilges, re-fuelling or repairing damaged fenders. The insatiable gulls were rooting about in the basin and outer harbour and not strutting up and down the quays impudently begging from the trippers. Cats lay in the sun without feeling threatened by car wheels.

Wycliffe lit his pipe and let the peace and the sun soak in. It was the first chance he had had to take a good look round the village and he intended to make the most of it. He came to the slipway where *Green Lady IV* was still supported on her cradle, the gaping hole in her side an indignity, almost an indecency. Pea-green, an unusual colour for a boat. Surely he had heard that the Cornish are superstitious about the colour green?

'The Owl and the Pussy-Cat went to sea
In a beautiful pea-green boat,
They took some honey and plenty of money,
Wrapped up in a five-pound note.'

Had Gill remembered the Owl and the Pussy-Cat?

Wycliffe knew about the murder what everyone else knew, what had been reported in the papers and on television and radio. Jimmy Gill, his deputy, had cleared it all up in a matter of days, which should do Jimmy a bit of good where it mattered. The chief constable had always had reservations about him.

'No real vision . . .' By which he meant, no imagination, but imagination is a dirty word in the force. 'A good thief catcher, a good detective I grant you, but a senior officer has to have that something extra . . .'

Perhaps this case would help to put the record straight.

He walked to the end of the eastern breakwater and back. The trippers were beginning to arrive. He spent most of the morning pottering about the harbour. A Midlander, born and bred, boats and the sea fascinated him. Although he now lived in sight of the sea he never tired of it. In any case this was different; the little harbour was alive. Pleasure boats running trips, a few remaining fishing boats, the self-drives with their putt-putt motors, the sailing dinghies with blue, red and white sails and even one or two craft which could claim to be yachts. A constant coming and going of row-boats and 'prams' ferrying between the steps and moorings, their owners rowing or sculling or sitting back and letting an outboard do the work.

One shabby little launch, its blue paint flaking, attracted his attention in particular. She was moored in the outer harbour among the larger craft. She was half-decked and in the well a boy and a girl were eating a meal using the top of the engine housing as a table. They had a large plate of boiled fish and chunks of bread which they dunked in the juice. The girl wore a bikini and the boy trunks. Both were bronzed, with sun-bleached hair and they looked like godlings. On the stern the name *Marie-Jo* had been newly painted in large, white, rather crude letters. Did they know that they were in paradise?

At mid-day he was wondering what he would do for lunch. Few of the hotel residents came in for lunch and he had no wish to eat alone in that bare, bright dining-room.

It was almost like starting on a case, when he tried to establish a pattern for his days which he would do his best to follow until the case was over.

There were crowds milling about now, day-trippers mostly and he could not help wondering why they came. The harbour was beautiful in the sunshine and the village itself was not entirely spoiled, but these harassed families with their bickering children had no eyes for either and merely scolded their way from ice-cream stall to gift shop and from gift shop to café before returning to their cars or to the coach which brought them.

He had to decide where to eat. There were plenty of cafés offering chips with everything but he did not like chips, then he caught sight of a more interesting menu outside the Robartes Arms and his decision was made.

The dining-room behind the bars was full and he had a drink in the public bar while he waited for a place. There were few customers, though to judge from the noise the saloon bar must have been crowded. Evidently the public was for the locals. Two men in blue jerseys played dominoes and Wycliffe sat near them, watching, but his presence was not acknowledged.

When his turn came for lunch he was sharing a table with a stocky little man in well-fitting tweeds. His hair was close-cropped and almost white but his smooth skin was as brown as an Indian's.

'On holiday?'

Wycliffe said that he was.

'I live here. As a matter of fact, I'm the local G.P.' He was tucking in to a lamb cutlet with boiled potatoes and cauliflower. 'Don't miss the soup, it's lentil done with orange and coriander. I eat here most days and they do you very well for the money.'

Wycliffe was usually wary of strangers who tried to strike up an acquaintance, but the doctor had an engaging ingenuousness which made it impossible to snub him.

'Been here long?'

'Since Saturday.'

'So you missed most of the excitement.'

'Excitement?'

'Our murder.'

'Oh, I read about it in the papers.'

'Funny business. I've lived in this village for nearly twenty-five years and I still don't understand half that goes on.' He broke off, 'I don't suppose you would join me in a bottle of wine, I make it a rule never to drink alone—'

'It would be a pleasure.'

'Good! You must try their hock, it really is a very good wine.' He signed to the waitress and ordered. 'As I was saying, the village families are introverted, some little thing starts off a feud that can go on for generations, simmering away. They thrive on it, it's the stuff of life. For some it's their only reason for living. I visit three sisters, old maids, all in their seventies and two of them have only communicated with each other through the third for twenty years. God knows what will happen if the third sister goes first. Ah, here's the wine. No, let my friend try it . . . Good, isn't it? I knew you would like it.'

'The man who was murdered,' Wycliffe said, feeling that he must say something, 'that seemed straightforward enough. They've arrested his son, haven't they? Presumably he couldn't wait for his father's money.'

The doctor sipped his wine and rolled it round his tongue like a connoisseur. 'But he didn't get it, did he? I mean he wouldn't have whether they arrested him or not. The old man left everything to his grandchild—skipped a generation. There's a rum family if you like. The Tremains. And this is the second murder in the family.'

'The *second*?' Wycliffe really was startled.

The doctor waved his table napkin airily. 'Oh, the other was twenty years back, not long after I came to the village. Young fellow—he must have been a nephew to the old man—strangled his girl-friend one Sunday afternoon up on the cliffs. Coronation year it was—fifty-three.'

'What happened to him?'

'They didn't hang him, his sentence was commuted, he got twenty-one years. With remission that brought it down to fourteen. Anyway, he came out several years back . . .' He broke off again while the waitress cleared Wycliffe's soup plate and brought the main course. He had ordered fricassée of chicken and the doctor looked at it disparagingly. 'You'd have done better with the lamb, that's just tarted-up hash. You're not doing justice to this bottle.'

'Where is he now?'

'What? Where is who?'

'The man who was sentenced for murder.'

'Oh, he's dead. I don't remember the details if indeed I ever heard them, but it was some sort of accident; a road smash, I think. He never came back here.' He glanced at the menu and frowned, 'Yes, I think I'll have the apple pie—with cream.'

When they parted they still had not exchanged names but the doctor said, 'I suppose I shall see you again? You won't do better.'

After lunch he strolled along the quay once more, watching the pleasure boats taking aboard the afternoon trippers. A tall, loose-limbed man came out of a shop, spotted Wycliffe and turned away smartly, walking off in the other direction. Dandy Wilson. Wycliffe knew him professionally, he worked the hotels up and down the country conning women of a certain age. As a result he had spent almost as much time in gaol as out. Now he was well over forty and running to fat with little left of that elegance of dress and deportment which had earned him his nick-name. Wycliffe wondered what he was doing; there could be few pickings for his sort in the village. But everybody needs a holiday.

Wycliffe set out for a walk along the cliffs but by the time he had reached the level of the cliff path his heart was pounding and he was out of breath. Depressed, he sat in the heather, looking down on the village and, before long, he fell asleep. He drowsed the afternoon away until after five o'clock then returned to the village by a different route which brought him down some steps almost into the hotel yard. He had a headache, he felt fragile and he had to tell himself that forty-eight is not elderly.

The proprietress was at the reception desk, a very thin lady of uncertain age with jet-black hair belied by a pattern of wrinkles and by faded brown eyes which no art could disguise. She had shrivelled lips which she moved as little as possible so that her refined speech sounded like the effort of an amateur ventriloquist.

'You have a visitor, Chief Superintendent.'

He did not notice the form of address until her arch manner reminded him that they had registered simply as Mr and Mrs Wycliffe. Either Gill or—

'Chief Inspector Gill is waiting in the lounge.'

Wycliffe went through to the lounge, which was empty except for Gill and a cloud of acrid smoke from one of his little black cheroots. Gill unfolded his great length from the chair and the two men greeted each other with warmth. They were not in the least alike but they worked well together, each the complement of the other.

When the preliminaries were over Wycliffe said, 'I thought you'd packed up and gone.'

'Came back to see you.' Gill's manner was self-conscious and embarrassed, quite uncharacteristic. 'I won't beat about the bush; I'm not satisfied with my case.' His rubbery features contorted into a grotesque expression of doubt. 'I've brought the file with me and I want you to take a look at it.'

Wycliffe had never seen him so diffident or so restrained. 'What's the matter? Has Mr Bellings been riding you?' Bellings was the deputy chief and he had little time for Gill.

'No, I've learnt to live with him. It's me. In the ordinary way I wouldn't trouble you, but you being here, on the spot . . .'

Wycliffe was puzzled. 'I'll read through the file, gladly, but what's the trouble? Do you think you've got the wrong man?'

Gill considered. 'No, I don't think we've got the wrong man, but there's been something odd about this case from the start. I've missed something important and I keep looking over my shoulder. You know what I mean?'

He was standing staring out of the big window which commanded a panoramic view of the whole bay.

'I've mentioned this to Mr Bellings.'

'There was no need, it could have stayed between us.'

'I know, but you might want to make a few enquiries on your own account and I don't want to drop you in the deep end.'

When Gill had gone Wycliffe took the bulky file up to his room. As he opened it he was confronted by an enlarged photograph of

94

the dead man's face, taken after death by a police photographer. Considering that the corpse must have been several days old the impression was astonishingly life-like. The beard hid a good deal of the skin which would have been parboiled and livid. The eyes were closed by large, finely wrinkled lids and in life he had probably looked out on the world through hooded eyes. A strong face, unyielding.

After an hour spent on the file he was convinced that Gill had a case and a very strong one. He summarized it on a sheet of hotel notepaper:

1. Harry Tremain was a wealthy man and Cedric had good reason to suppose that he would inherit.

2. Cedric is in debt and twice, during the past six months, he has tried to defraud his father in the running of the garage. Gill suspected but could not prove that Cedric was being blackmailed.

3. Cedric has a reputation as a wild man, too ready with his fists when drunk, which is often.

4. The explosives used in the crime were stolen from the local quarry where Cedric was employed for a number of years, until, in fact, he was sacked for persistent brawling.

5. Cedric is a good mechanic and the preparation of a timed explosive device is probably within the limits of his skill.

6. On the Sunday afternoon prior to the explosion Cedric was working on the engine of the launch at his father's request.

7. Gill's men found in Cedric's private garage, among a lot of rubbish, a detonator, some lengths of copper wire and part of an alarm clock which could have come from the one used in the explosion.

On the face of it, an open and shut case. But Wycliffe had too much respect for Gill to write off his concern as no more than an attack of the jitters.

At a little before seven Helen arrived, looking a picture of health with hair bleached and skin tanned by the sun and wind.

'What's happened? You look better than you've looked for weeks.'

It was useless to try to hide anything from her.

Chapter Seven

THE FOLLOWING MORNING, after seeing Helen off, he drove to the county hospital where Dr Franks, the pathologist, had his laboratory. He had decided to retrace the main lines of the investigation and to see what turned up.

He dropped his photograph of the dead man on the bench where Franks was working.

'We got rid of him on Friday. Your lot had finished with him. Anyway, what are you doing here? I thought you were supposed to be ill. Wet-nursing for Gill, is that it?'

The two men had been friends for several years, both were much concerned with the consequences of violence but they had been affected differently. Wycliffe, hating any form of violence, saw it as wholly destructive, the final negation of humanity. Franks did not agree. 'It's part of the pattern, Charles,' he was fond of saying, 'the necessary complement of our capacity for love and tenderness. The humanity you talk about is compounded of both.' Franks was smug in his acceptance of his contentment with life. His smooth, round little person, always immaculate, radiated satisfaction.

'Tell me about him.'

'I've made a report.'

'I know, I've read it.'

Franks removed a slide from the microscope he had been using and pencilled a note on the label. 'His head and the upper part of his trunk were virtually undamaged, his legs took the blast. He must have been standing on the thing and when it blew he went up like a rocket.' He made an expressive gesture.

'Like some coffee?'

'Please.'

'Then come along to my office.'

His office was white from floor to ceiling, more like a surgery or even an operating theatre, and the impression was sustained by the metal furniture which had about it a suggestion of the dental chair and the operating table. Even his secretary, one of a long line of young girls to fill the post, wore white.

'You remember Tessa? . . . No? . . . Is it so long since you paid me a visit, you old rascal?' He turned to the girl. 'Coffee, Tessa, black for the superintendent and no sugar.'

Wycliffe was always a little shocked by Franks's affairs with girls young enough to be his daughters and, deep down, a little envious too. What must it be like? How did he manage it? When a girl applies for a job you can hardly ask her whether . . . Yet it always seemed to work.

Franks opened a drawer in his desk and took out a specimen tube containing fragments of metal.

'His feet and legs below the knee were blasted and his thighs and groin were peppered with these. Bits of cast iron.' He rattled the tube. 'I sent most of them to Gill. If you ask me the charge must have been packed in a bit of cast-iron pipe or something of the sort to increase the effect of the blast.'

'There was little damage to the launch away from the site of the explosion.'

'I'm not surprised, but what are you getting at?'

'Just that if he hadn't been standing over the engine he probably wouldn't have been killed.'

Franks pulled at the tip of his pink little nose, 'I see what you mean; it would be a chancy way to commit a murder.'

'Exactly, that is what I thought, but you have more experience of explosives.'

Tessa came in with the coffee. Franks added an artificial sweetener to his and stirred. 'Of course, it's quite possible that the thing was triggered to go off when he performed a particular act, say, when he lifted the lid of the engine housing. I suppose he could be relied on to do that at least once in the course of the trip?'

'Then why bother with a clock? Here, you'd better read this. It's the report on the explosion from Forensic.'

Franks glanced through the tedious length of the report, reading bits aloud:

'. . . sunk by an explosive charge placed near the engine housing on the port side beneath the bottom boards . . . The charge was almost certainly detonated electrically through a timing device . . . Fragments of a clockwork mechanism were found which have been identified as parts of a 30-hour alarm clock of a type mass-produced by Timecal and distributed through chain stores . . . There is no evidence to show that the device was in any way connected with the engine or that it formed part of a "booby-trap" . . . evidence that a dry battery was employed . . . In our opinion the charge consisted of approximately two pounds of blasting gelatine.'

Franks pushed the report back across the desk. 'If that's the case the murderer was lucky, he probably over-estimated the effect of the charge. People often do.'

'Or he may not necessarily have wanted to kill the old man.'

'If he meant it as a warning it wasn't very friendly.'

Tessa was typing away on her white, electric typewriter, her fingers held almost horizontally to avoid damaging her nails.

They chatted for a while then Wycliffe drove slowly back to the village through a maze of narrow lanes. The hedges were garish with white ramsons and red campions. After only one false turn he came out at the top of a hill with a distant prospect of the sea and began the slow descent. First, the camping site, largely screened by elms; then the slopes peppered with new houses; a row of old-fashioned council houses and the cemetery, then the beginning of the village proper. The hill became steeper and narrowed between rows of terraced houses which ended, finally, in the square.

The village was crowded and he could find nowhere to park his car until, after weaving his way through the narrow streets, he arrived back at his hotel.

The fact that Harry Tremain had been killed by the explosion was apt to obscure the fact that time-bombs as weapons of

99

discriminate murder are notoriously unreliable. A good many tyrants, including Hitler, have survived to punish their would-be assassins. It could be argued that the intending killer had, as Franks suggested, imagined that his bomb would be more destructive than it turned out to be. But Wycliffe found it difficult to believe that a man capable of making such a weapon should be ignorant of its variable potential. But why would anyone run the risk of putting a bomb aboard the old man's launch unless they wanted to kill him? Merely to sink the launch? There seemed to be no sense in that.

Already he was beginning to feel sympathy with Gill's uneasiness.

He went to his room and replaced the photograph and the report in Gill's file. He would never have admitted it but for the first time since the start of his enforced holiday he was beginning to enjoy himself. He was indulging in that most delectable kind of pleasure which is both anticipatory and lightly spiced with guilt. Yesterday he had felt tantalizingly excluded from the community of the village, a spectator on the outside, now with this drab-looking file he was licensed to become a privileged interloper. Now, if he wanted to, he could probe into their lives; winkle out their secrets.

Often, at the start of a case, he would savour the prospect as one might turn the pages of a new autobiography or take a peep into a bundle of someone else's letters. The chance to live vicariously in other people's skins; for him, one of the attractions of the job. He knew it to be unworthy and salved his conscience with the reflection that he was rarely censorious, never malicious though always insatiably curious.

'Eunice Williams, née Tremain. 41. Daughter of deceased.' In the file Gill had pencilled against her name, 'Shrewd and bitchy.'

Wycliffe knew The Quay House where she lived, the gaunt, slate-fronted building at the end of the wharf. From the window of his hotel room he could see its blue-grey roof of Delabole slate rising above those of the other houses. He decided to pay her and it a visit; he would talk to her but he would also see where the murdered man had spent his whole life.

It was the hottest day of the year, so far, with no breath of air, and the waterfront was crowded with people, many of the men in bathing trunks and the girls in bikinis. There were queues for ice-cream and for drinks and as he threaded his way through he felt slightly superior because, he told himself, he was doing a job.

A whole flight of steps led up to the front door of The Quay House and the door itself stood open to a well-scrubbed stone-flagged passage. A huge tabby cat was stretched out asleep on the threshold. There was no bell and no knocker so he banged on the door with his knuckles. A tall, bony woman with wispy fair hair and a bulging forehead stepped out of a room at the far end of the passage. She did not come to the door but called, 'Yes?'

'Mrs Williams? Mrs Eunice Williams?'

'That's right, what do you want?'

Wycliffe introduced himself and she frowned. 'You'd better go into the sitting-room, I'll be with you in a minute.'

He stepped over the cat and entered the sitting-room. It was dimly lit through a narrow gap in the red velvet curtains and it took some time for his eyes to accommodate to the gloom. The room was large, the floor covered with a threadbare carpet which had once had an elaborate floral pattern. The furniture was Edwardian and looked as though it had come from a second-hand store before the craze for renovation set in.

Eunice arrived, buttoning a blue, nylon housecoat. She had run a comb through her hair, dabbed powder on her cheeks and smeared lipstick on her lips.

Wycliffe expressed sorrow at her bereavement but she was unresponsive.

'Yes, well, there it is. What do you want? Is there something new?'

'Just one or two questions, Mrs Williams.'

She had perched herself on the edge of a sofa upholstered in red velvet from which most of the nap had long since disappeared. She could not relax or even sit still but Wycliffe felt sure that this had nothing to do with his visit. She was the kind of woman who must always be 'doing' and she almost certainly kept the house in a constant state of turmoil with her cleaning.

'Questions! All I've had is questions. It was bad enough father getting killed, then they have to accuse my brother—'

Wycliffe spoke soothingly. 'Somebody killed your father.'

'I don't believe it. It must have been some sort of accident.' But she did not sound convinced.

'The evidence for murder is overwhelming.'

She examined her hands, reddened by scouring and scrubbing. 'You're new. What do you want to ask me?'

'You evidently do not believe that your brother is guilty so I must ask you, did your father have any enemies?'

'That's what the others asked me. Why should he have enemies in a village where he lived all his life?'

'He was well off.'

'He wasn't short but—'

'And you and your brother expected to inherit?'

Two little spots of colour flamed on her cheeks. 'And didn't we have every reason? What sort of father would leave all he'd got to a grandchild? And to one grandchild. I've got a child too! To leave it all to that . . . that slut, it's an insult, that's what it is!' Her emotion brought tears and she dabbed her eyes under the big lenses.

'Your father went out to see his crab-pots on Monday morning. Was that his usual routine?'

She brushed back a wisp of hair from her forehead. 'Unless it was rough weather.' She added after a moment, 'He didn't have to do it, he just couldn't bear the thought of giving up his boat.'

'But anyone of his acquaintance would know that he would be out seeing to his pots between six and seven on an average morning?'

She frowned, wrinkling the almost transparent skin of her forehead. 'Well, no. I mean, it depends on the tide, doesn't it?'

Wycliffe had constantly to be reminded that for many who live by the sea, tides matter more than clocks.

'What I mean is that they would know that he would be out as soon as there was enough water in the basin.' She pulled her coat down in an effort to cover her white bony knees.

'What did you think when you heard that the launch had blown up?'

'Think? I thought that there must have been something wrong with the engine, a petrol leak or something like that.'

'Don't these marine engines run on paraffin?'

'They start on petrol, then switch over.' She was pulling at a thread from one of the buttons on her coat. 'He mentioned that he was having trouble with the fuel intake, or he thought that was what it was. Cedric spent Sunday afternoon working on her. He came in while we were having tea on Sunday afternoon and said everything was all right.'

'Were your father and Cedric on good terms?'

She looked at him sharply. 'What are you getting at now?'

'Merely asking a question.'

'Well, Cedric got on with his father about as well as most sons do, no better and no worse.'

The sun had come round and was now streaming through the gap in the curtains making a narrow golden path across the shabby carpet and dividing the room in two.

'I would like to see your father's room.'

She looked surprised. 'His room? Again? What for? They've been up there—'

Wycliffe did not answer and after a brief pause she stood up.

The passage seemed ablaze with sunlight after the darkened room. The stairs at the end were broad and elegantly turned but the carpet was worn through in places and it had lost all semblance of pattern. Four or five doors opened off the first landing and she went to one and pushed it open.

'I'm afraid the room is in a state, just as he left it. He would never let me in here to do anything and the other detective said we mustn't touch anything till we heard.' She was on the defensive, assuming a brittle nonchalance of manner to cover her nervousness.

103

'Did you break the lock, Mrs Williams?'

She looked down at the splintered wood of the door-jamb where the fixing screws had been prized out. 'Oh, the lock, my husband did that. I mean, we had to get in.'

'Your father kept his room locked?'

'Always, and he carried the key about with him. But we had to see what was in there, didn't we? I mean, we weren't to know they would find the body so soon.'

The room had two windows, one facing the wharf and the other across the harbour and out to sea with a view along the cliffs away to the right. Harry Tremain had had a grandstand view of everything that went on.

Wycliffe had not seen such a room since childhood. There was a double bed with brass rails and knobs, a mahogany wardrobe with a full-length mirror let into the door, a chest-of-drawers and a washstand with a semi-circular, white, marble top. On the wash-stand stood a large ewer and basin of china, decorated with red roses, and a soap drain. Underneath, on a little raised platform, were two chamber-pots to match. Incongruously, against one wall, there was a roll-topped desk with a swivel chair in front of it. The wallpaper had faded beyond the possibility of discerning any pattern and the carpet had lost almost all of its pile. An easy chair was placed so as to command a view from both windows and there was a pair of binoculars on the chest-of-drawers. The room was permeated with the smell of stale tobacco smoke and there was a row of pipes in a rack above the desk. A heavy reefer coat hung from a nail behind the door.

'I suppose he spent a lot of time up here?'

She sniffed. 'When he wasn't out or eating his food he was up here. If I'd been fool enough to wait on him he'd have had his meals up here.'

Her temples were a network of fine, blue veins and the skin below her eyes was purple as though bruised. She ran a finger over the top of the desk and looked with disgust at the grime it collec-ted. 'He was a difficult man, obstinate. Nothing was ever to his liking.'

There was an oil painting, a portrait, hanging over the bed, ornately framed in gilt. A head and shoulders of a man in middle age wearing the inevitable blue jersey and peaked cap. A strong face with a prominent chin accentuated by a fringe of black beard following the line of the jaw-bone.

'A man who used to live across the harbour, an artist, did that for him. He was flattered. God knows what he paid for it.'

Wycliffe rolled back the lid of the desk. It was almost empty, a cheap writing pad, a few envelopes, a cheque-book and a clip of bills interleaved with cancelled cheques. He flicked through them. Fuel, groceries, milk, television rental, rates—

She was watching him closely. 'We looked after him so it was only right he should pay some of the bills. It was all he did do. Although he was my own father I've got to say that he was mean.'

Wycliffe said nothing and she went on:

'Geoff, that's my husband, doesn't earn a lot and we can't afford a car although he has to go in and out to town every day. I asked father if he would help us to get a little car, and do you know what he said? He said that the bus had always been good enough for him and if we were short of money why didn't we take in visitors like mother did.'

Wycliffe looked round the room. No books, no television or radio. The old man must have sat in his chair, smoking his pipe and watching the world outside. He would have had plenty of time to reflect on his family, perhaps to gloat over how he would leave his money.

'Did he never go out except to see to his pots?'

'He'd walk the length of the wharf a couple of times a day. He used to go to chapel. In fact, he was a local preacher but he gave it all up after mother died.'

'Did he never leave the village?'

'Once a fortnight he would catch the bus into town to go to the bank and the first Saturday in every month he would go there, but what for I've no more idea than you have.'

'You mean that on the first Saturday in every month he would catch the bus into town?'

'That's what I said.'

'Did you ever ask him why?'

She sniffed. 'It would have been a waste of words.'

'How long had these monthly visits been going on?'

'Years.'

'Did they start before your mother died?'

A curious little smile. 'Long before.'

There were footsteps on the stairs, a child's, and Eunice hurried out on to the landing. 'Be careful, Peter! Mummy told you to stay in the garden.'

A pale, thin little boy came into the room, four or five years old. He had black hair and large, dark eyes and Wycliffe could not help being reminded of an appeal for Oxfam.

'This is Peter. Say "hallo" to the gentleman, Peter.'

The child merely looked at Wycliffe with a steadfast gaze and held his mother's hand. Eunice swept his slender little body up into her arms and kissed him. 'Who's mummy's little man, then?'

There could be no doubt that Eunice had found a target for her love.

Wycliffe was groping idly in the drawers of the desk and he came up with a large manilla envelope containing a score or more of photographs. He slid them out on to the desk and shuffled through them. All sorts and sizes, some of them nearly bleached, others in a sharp contrast of black and white; a few with a fuzzy background of classical props from some photographer's studio of the twenties. Eunice stood by, watching him with seeming indifference. Peter, back on his feet, wandered over to one of the windows.

A snapshot of Eunice as a girl, unmistakeable. Harry Tremain and his wife as a young couple looking fixedly at the camera with strained smiles. A stocky youth in a suit which was on the point of splitting at the seams, a young bull, ready for stud.

'Cedric?'

She nodded.

Then a postcard, a studio portrait of another youth, thin and staring at the camera with weak eyes.

'Who is that?'

'A cousin of mine.'

Something in the tone of her voice made him look at her. She was suddenly tense.

'Don't do that, Peter, you'll get your jersey filthy!' Peter was resting with his arms on the window ledge, watching the people on the quay.

'The cousin who murdered his sweetheart?' Wycliffe was deliberately cruel.

It was startling to see her white face and neck suffuse with colour. She nodded.

'What happened to him?'

'He went to prison.'

'But afterwards, when he came out?'

She made an effort. 'I heard that he had been killed in a motor accident.'

'You never saw him again?'

'No.'

'And his father and mother, what about them?'

'His mother left the village when he was—when they sentenced him.'

'And his father?'

'Sidney Tremain, my father's brother, hanged himself when Morley was ten.' She spoke with a curious air of defiance which he failed to understand.

Wycliffe gathered the photographs back into their envelope and changed the subject.

'Mrs Williams, if your brother did not kill his father there must be someone with a terrible grudge against him.'

She became more agitated, so that she put her bony knuckles in her mouth like a child to hold back tears.

'A detonator and parts of a clock similar to the one used in the crime were found in his garage.'

She shook her head slowly but said nothing. She was obviously on tenterhooks waiting for him to go and he allowed himself to be led down the stairs to the stone passage. Peter followed behind. In the passage he paused.

'What about your niece, Laura, did she see much of your father?'

Eunice had regained some of her composure. 'She used to come here to suck up to him, lolling around in the chairs showing everything she'd got. It's easy to see now what she was after but you wouldn't think a man of sixty-five—'

He was turning away when a new thought struck him. 'Could your father swim?'

'Swim? Not a stroke.'

'Isn't that unusual for a man who spent his whole life by the sea?'

For the first time he saw the ghost of a smile. 'Not really. Most of the older men round here can't swim. If you ask them they'll tell you they don't reckon on falling in.'

He thanked her, stepped over the sleeping cat who seemed scarcely to have moved a muscle, and left.

People were milling about on the quay and now there were queues outside the cafés for lunch. The sky, still cloudless, had taken on a brazen hue and it seemed to be even hotter.

Seeing the queues made him give up the idea of lunch. He went to a telephone box and asked to be put through to his area headquarters on a reversed charge call. He spoke to Sergeant Bourne who was in charge of records, a young man of the new breed, a graduate with a very clear idea of his merit and prospects.

'I want the file on Morley Tremain, who was sentenced for the murder of his girl-friend—'

'I think that must have been before my time, sir.'

'I think you're probably right, Bourne; the crime was committed in 1953.'

'But that will be in the stack!'

'I dare say. I want you to get it out and to send it to me.'

'By dispatch, sir?'

'Post will do.'

The 'stack' was accommodated in an underground vault where

there was less than six feet of head room and hundreds of yards of metal shelving stacked with files. The place was poorly lit, dusty and a haunt of spiders.

He came out of the telephone box and went across to the Robartes Arms with the intention of having a drink and, perhaps, a sandwich, in the bar.

There were a few more customers in the public bar than on the previous day. The domino players and their supporters seemed to be fixtures but there was also a foursome playing darts and a critical audience watching them. Wycliffe collected his drink and joined the critics. Three of the players belonged to the cap and jersey brigade but the fourth wore a suit, he was tall, very thin and his face was horribly disfigured. 'Walter' they called him and his skill drew frequent cries of admiration from the spectators.

'Look at that! You can't play against that ... Walt's a bloody marvel when it comes to darts ... Double eighteen and he's home ... There, what did I tell you? Bloody marvellous!'

The tall man turned away from the board, picked up his drink and modestly endured the congratulations of his friends. Wycliffe could not help looking at his face; the flesh had the texture and colour of putty and was criss-crossed by a tangle of scars; his mouth was twisted and his lower eyelids were pulled down exposing the red rims. He wore glasses and an obvious wig which accentuated his grotesque appearance. He stared at Wycliffe, the only stranger present, as disfigured people sometimes do, seeming to challenge some response.

Now that the darts game was over conversation started up.

'Busy at the site, Walter?'

'Full up, as we have been since the beginning of last month.'

'Weather's holding.'

One of the cap-and-jerseys looked briefly out of the door. 'Change coming.'

The barman came out from behind his counter and approached Wycliffe. He spoke very quietly. 'Dr Langley has saved your place if you would like to go through, sir.'

'Dr Langley has saved your place—' He hardly knew whether

to be annoyed or pleased but he went through to the dining-room where the doctor was sitting at the same table as before, smiling a welcome.

'Braised liver, that's what I'm having and if it's up to their usual standard I can recommend it. The soup, today, is tomato, out of a tin, so we can give that a miss ... You've no objection to onion with the liver?'

'None.'

'Good! What shall we have with it, then, a claret?'

'Why not?'

The little doctor's brown eyes were twinkling. 'You didn't tell me yesterday that you were here officially.'

'Officially? What do you mean?'

'Mrs Borlase, the female dragon who runs your hotel, has an arthritic knee.'

'I'm here on holiday.' Wycliffe was at his most stolid. But his ill humour could hardly survive the doctor's irrepressible bonhomie.

'When I was in the bar just now there was a chap playing darts, a man with a terrible facial disfigurement—'

'Walter Tyson, he's a sort of manager at the camping site up the hill. The farmer, Joe Lidgey, who owns it, put him in there two years ago.'

'A local?'

The doctor shook his head. 'Newcomer; came here on holiday, liked the place and stayed.'

'What happened to his face?'

'I don't know the details but I understand that he was thrown out of a car through the windscreen into a pool of burning petrol.'

'He seems to have been accepted in the public bar.'

'The darts did that for him; good passport even here.' The doctor poured himself a glass of wine and held it to the light, admiring the rich reflections. 'He was friendly with your dead man, he used to go out in the launch now and then. Decent sort of chap; quiet. He lives in one of the permanent caravans but it must be a lonely life, especially in the winter.' The doctor paused then asked, 'Do you really think Cedric did it?'

Wycliffe did not want to be churlish so he merely shook his head and said nothing, but he wondered what the doctor's reaction would have been if a comparative stranger asked him, 'Do you really think you did your best for that patient?'

But Wycliffe's silence did not deter him.

'In some ways Cedric has been his own worst enemy. He's crude, self-indulgent, quarrelsome, violent on occasion but he's not the sort to bear a grudge—'

'He's been charged but he hasn't been convicted,' Wycliffe said in a tone which he hoped would close the discussion.

Chapter Eight

AFTER LUNCH HE walked as far as The Quay House, then back through the main street which was so narrow that it rarely saw the sun. The shops were prosperous, expensive and either twee or blatantly vulgar. Home-made cakes and pyramids of glutinous fudge sheltered behind small, square panes of bow-fronted shops; paintings by local artists crowded small windows and display cases tempting the visitor into galleries up rickety flights of stairs. There were 'antique' shops selling fairground ornaments of the twenties and open-fronted gift shops which looked like a Cecil B. de Mille version of Aladdin's cave. Crocodiles of tourists worked their way up one side of the street and down the other taking refuge in shop doorways whenever a van tried to edge its way through.

He was looking for the stone-shop run by Cedric's wife:

'Julie Tremain, née Bray. 39. Wife of Cedric. Separated May 1973. Rents shop in main street with living accommodation over and runs business in polished stones.'

Gill had annotated the report for his benefit: 'Elegant female; keeps her cool and her figure. Apparently not vindictive.'

He found the shop. The window was crowded with bracelets, rings and necklaces of mounted 'local' stones. There were trays of polished and unpolished stones for the do-it-yourself addict and a couple of tumbling machines. While he stood, looking in, a woman of about forty, wearing a paisley blouse, reached into the window for a tray of stones. Their eyes met. She had good features as well as a good figure, high cheekbones, large, dark eyes and her black hair framed her face as though it enjoyed doing it. How had Cedric drawn such a trump out of the pack?

He passed the corner shop where he had taken up to buy his

tobacco and his morning paper; the shop which, though he did not know it, had once belonged to the Sidney Tremains. Unlike most of the others it had changed little in twenty years but the fascia board carried a new name and the white-enamelled letters advertising Fry's chocolate had finally disappeared from the shop door.

He reached the square, where a policeman was directing the traffic. Across the square there was a row of petrol pumps and Cedric's garage. In the forecourt of the garage he could see Dandy Wilson's tall figure; he seemed to be in conversation with one of the garage hands. Wycliffe liked the square, there was room to move. Women in brief summer dresses were gossiping in groups and inspecting the goods displayed in front of the shops. Everybody was telling everybody else what glorious weather they were having but adding that it wouldn't last.

Wycliffe crossed the square and turned up the hill out of the village. He climbed the steep slope between the terraced houses and passed the recreation ground and the cemetery. Although his whole body was bathed in perspiration he was glad to find that his pulse-rate and breathing seemed almost back to normal. Above the cemetery a road, which had not been properly made up, led off to the left: *Treslothan Road*, where Cedric lived. The houses were detached, about five years old, the sort with two bathrooms, garage for a car and a Mini, and a little cloakroom with a loo off the hall. Central heating, of course.

Gill, honest even when it hurt, had noted, 'Cedric was a tearaway as a youngster and he hasn't changed, but, to some extent, it's been a case of giving a dog a bad name ... Weak, quick tempered and violent, but is he cold-bloodedly vicious?' A good question.

The gardens had hedges of *Escallonia* now spattered with flowers like drops of blood. The bees were busy and somebody was mowing a lawn. The houses faced the sea, looking out over the tremendous sweep of the bay. The houses on his right presented their fronts to the road while those on his left offered their backs. Cedric's was on the left, less well cared for than the others; the gravelled sweep from the gate was overgrown with weeds and the woodwork of the house needed paint. There were two cars parked on the gravel, a Jaguar, grey with dust and showing signs of rust, and a fierce looking MG, in a brilliant red.

Wycliffe was sauntering along, smoking his pipe, getting back the taste of it after a period of deprivation. The up-and-over door of Cedric's garage had not been opened for some time, grass and dandelions flourished along the base, but it was in Cedric's garage that Gill's men had found the detonator, bits of a clock and lengths of copper wire. A very convenient and lucky find. Was Cedric such a bloody fool? Probably. But there must be another way into the garage, either from the house or from the front garden, for the big door had not been opened in months.

One of the double gates of the drive was off its hinges and lying against the hedge. Wycliffe walked in and round the side of the house to the front. A large lawn with grass in dire need of cutting stretched down to a hedge of tamarisk. Beyond that a few maritime pines grew among the gravestones in the cemetery, crooked against the sky.

On this side the garage had an ordinary door with a glass panel. He tried it, it was not locked.

'Looking for me?'

A girl was walking across the grass towards him. 'I'm Laura Tremain.'

Wycliffe, feeling a little foolish, started to introduce himself but she forestalled him.

'Detective Chief Superintendent Wycliffe, I know. News travels fast in this village. As a matter of fact I was coming to see you.'

She had been sunbathing and she wore a floral bikini and a short, matching jacket. The same features, the same dark eyes and caressing hair as her mother but twenty years younger with the bloom of youth still fresh.

Laura Tremain had appeared in Gill's report: '21. Daughter of Cedric. Employed by a firm of accountants. Said to be on intimate terms with her boss who is a married man with two grown-up children.' Gill had not added one of his asides. If he had it would probably have been, 36.22.34.

'Hot isn't it?' She glanced up at the sky which was assuming a coppery hue though there was no obvious cloud. 'I think we must be in for a storm. Would you like a drink?'

He followed her into the house, into a large room with windows at both ends. A pleasant room with a tweedy carpet and upholstery, comfortable and not over furnished. She left him for a moment or two then came back with cans of beer and glasses. There was mist on the cans, which must have come straight from the refrigerator.

'Lager all right for you?'

Her body was uniformly brown. She had long, slim thighs and firm breasts in no need of uplift. She seemed entirely relaxed, in fact he had the impression that she was watching him with half-amused tolerance. For his part he was very conscious of her body, which made him wonder if, at heart, he was a dirty old man or merely a normal male. Twenty-five years' acquaintance with the seamy side of life had not helped him to resolve such questions which troubled the depths of his rather prim soul.

He opened the beer.

'You live here?'

'Where else?'

'I had assumed that you lived with your mother.'

She offered him a box of cigarettes and when he refused, took one herself.

'No, that wouldn't have suited mother or me; two women in that poky little flat over the shop. And dad doesn't bother me, he learned a long time ago that it's best to leave me alone. In any case it suits him to have me here. I cook a meal for him occasionally and I run the vacuum over the place before it gets up to his ankles.'

She smoked like a man, holding the cigarette between her lips and narrowing her eyes against the smoke.

'You said that you were coming to see me, why?'

'Well, it's pretty obvious that the police are having second thoughts about my father.'

Wycliffe put on his best cow-like expression. 'It is quite usual for an investigation to continue after an arrest has been made, so please don't read anything into that.'

She was unimpressed. 'Well, anyway, you're a new man, taking a fresh look. What did you come here for if you—?'

'Did you expect your grandfather to leave his money to you?'

She looked surprised. 'Christ, no! It creased me.'

'Was he generous to you while he was alive?'

She stopped to think. 'Yes, I suppose he was, really quite generous. He would slip me a fiver now and then when I went to see him and he bought me the car—the MG, although I wasn't allowed to tell anybody. Aunt Eunice thought it was part of my immoral earnings.'

'There was some difficulty in finding his will, how did it reach you?'

'It came through the post from his bank, four days after his death.' She got up. 'I'll show you.' She went out and he heard her going upstairs.

She came down a few minutes later and handed him a letter written in a large, spidery hand.

Dear Laura,

I have told the bank to send you this packet containing my will four days after I am dead. Cedric and Eunice have had four days to think about it and to wonder whether they would be better off or worse without a will. Well now they will know. The only pleasure you get from people waiting for you to die is to make sure they don't get it. So I am leaving it all to you except the house which is for Eunice. I don't think anybody would get Eunice out. She is like her mother. You get all my investments and the property I have left and the garage. I hope you will let your father stay on there but you will have to watch him for his own good. He is very weak and that has got him into enough trouble. But he is still my son and your father. As far back as I can go the Tremains have always been a funny lot. Some weak and wild like your father and others hard and greedy like your aunt Eunice. Things arnt always what they seem not by a long way and you may find out about it one day. But it is always best for the family to stick together. You should remember that. You are a Tremain all right but you arnt weak and you arnt greedy so I thought you was the best one. Be a good girl and dont show this to anybody only the will.

Your loving grandfather

Harry Tremain

PS   Dont let some lofer marry you for your money they will be after you now.

Wycliffe handed the letter back. 'Why show this to me?'

'I should have thought that was obvious. He's hinting at something fishy.'

Wycliffe said, dully, 'You think so?'

She frowned with impatience. 'Of course I think so. There's something he was covering up—'

'Whatever it was, it might not help your father.'

'Father didn't kill him, I'm quite sure of that. He's got a hot temper and he might kill somebody in a fight or in a sudden crisis but he wouldn't—he couldn't, plan a cold-blooded murder. In any case, where did he learn to make a bomb?'

'You know what was found in the garage of this house?'

'Planted!' She was disdainful. 'The place is never locked and there's nobody here most of the time.'

'And who would want to incriminate your father?'

'Surely that's up to you to find out?' She brushed ash from her midriff with a muttered imprecation.

Gill had interrogated Cedric personally.

'I understand that you did some work on the engine of your father's boat the day before he was killed.'

'Sunday afternoon; that's right. He was always buggering about with it, upsetting the timing or the mixture, then he'd have trouble and I'd have to sort it out.'

117

'How long did it take you?'

'Not long. I went down about half-three. She was moored off so I had to get out to her but I was back in father's kitchen by the time they was having their tea—say about five or a quarter past.'

'Did anybody see you working on the boat?'

'Half the village and a couple of thousand bloody trippers, I should think.'

'I was thinking of somebody close at hand, able to see what you were doing.'

'If you don't bloody well believe—'

'Just answer my questions, it will be better for everybody if you do.'

'You think I fixed some gadget . . . Anyway, Toby Curnow was working on his boat and she was laying alongside. We were chatting on and off, he can tell you.'

Without realizing it Wycliffe had taken his pipe out and was lighting it. 'Do you mind?'

She dismissed the question with a gesture.

'Are you fond of your father?'

She frowned. He recognized something which he had observed in his own children, an innate honesty unimpaired by conventional forms. As a young man, faced with the same question, he would have answered automatically, 'Of course!' He did not know whether or not the change was for the better.

'Not fond, exactly, he's been a bit of a bastard, especially to mother, but I feel that I owe him something. He could have been a lot worse.'

Gill had asked Cedric: 'Did you take anything aboard with you?'

'Nothing.'

'No tools?'

'I said nothing and I meant bloody nothing. There's a set of spanners and screwdrivers aboard.'

'I suppose you've thought a lot about how the explosion which killed your father was contrived?'

118

'I heard that they've found bits of a clock.'

'I heard that too.' Wycliffe could imagine Gill's expression when he said this. 'You once worked in the quarry?'

'Once.'

'Do you know something about explosives?'

'Anybody who's worked in a quarry knows something about explosives, even if it's only to bloody well leave 'em alone, but laying a charge and pulling a plunger is a very different story from making a bloody time-bomb, believe you me. In any case, you may have noticed that a clock goes round once in twelve hours and this one must have popped off about seven in the morning so that lets me out.'

'Not necessarily, a clock can be modified, it's been done.'

'Not by me it hasn't; I'm a mechanic not a bloody clock-maker.'

Wycliffe had read the verbatim report, a bald record of the interrogation. He wished that he had been there to follow the changing expressions on Cedric's face, to note his pauses, to spot the times when he was reluctant to speak and those when he had been in too much hurry. But he had to admit that, such as it was, the report had left him with a favourable impression of Cedric.

'According to the report, your father spent the night of Sunday, prior to your grandfather's death, with his mistress.'

A faint smile, presumably at his use of the word 'mistress'. 'Elaine spent the night here if that's what you're getting at.'

'*Here?*' The report had not made that clear.

Elaine Ritter's evidence was the only really weak point in Gill's case. If it was true that she had spent the night with Cedric it was unlikely that he had had an opportunity to return to *Green Lady IV* and plant the bomb. So, if he had not modified the clock mechanism and put it aboard on Sunday afternoon he was in the clear. The prosecution would rely on discrediting Elaine Ritter, who had a reputation for living on her wits and her sex.

Laura was looking at him with the same half-smile which was beginning to irritate. It was as though she were initiating him into the ways of the world.

'Elaine often came here, she lives in one of the permanent

caravans on the site and I don't imagine that is very convenient.'

'And she spent the Sunday night here?'

She nodded. 'Elaine arrived just before ten on Sunday evening and the two of us had breakfast together next morning before father was out of bed.'

'You . . . you get on with her?'

'Why not?'

'Could your father have gone out and returned during the night without your knowledge?'

'Of course, but I doubt if he could have done so without Elaine knowing.'

He must have remained silent for some time and the girl was looking at him with a tolerant expression.

'What sort of man was your grandfather?'

She considered the question. 'I suppose he was what his women made him, first his wife then his daughter. I didn't know granny when she was younger but, from what I hear, she must have been very like Aunt Eunice.'

'You think that men are always what women make them?'

'Mostly, yes.'

'What about your young man?'

'He's not young, he's coming on for your age and he's married with two children, one of them older than I am.'

'Your boss?'

'How clever of you.'

That dart found its mark.

She came out, as she was, on to the gravelled drive to see him off and as he was leaving she called after him, 'By the way, did you want something in the garage?'

'What? No, no thank you.'

He felt disgruntled and irritable and he was passing the cemetery before he began to see the funny side and was able to laugh at himself.

Twenty-four hours earlier he had known about the case only what everyone else knew, what he had read in the newspapers. Then Gill had brought his report which had filled in a mass of detail. So much detail that he had become confused. What had seemed, at first sight, a straightforward case had acquired ramifications. Now, at least, the people mentioned in Gill's report were coming alive. Eunice and the girl in particular, but the dead man and Cedric were also emerging as people in their own right. Not merely as black-and-white characters in a drama of victim and suspect, but as people leading more or less normal lives with no sense of being predestined for notoriety.

And people kept telling him that Cedric could not have killed his father. His sister, Eunice, his daughter and, more significantly, the doctor. '... self-indulgent, quarrelsome, violent on occasion, but not the sort to bear a grudge.' Even Gill had his doubts, otherwise he would not have come to Wycliffe.

He had been walking and taking little count of his surroundings, so that the first lightning flash startled him. He looked up at the sky and was surprised to see that leaden clouds seemed to have condensed out of the great copper dome of an hour before. It was no less hot, he was aware of the sweat beneath his arms and of his shirt sticking to his back, and when the first drops of rain came, large drops which made circular patches on the pavement, they were warm. He wondered whether the storm would make the sea rough and where Helen was.

Thunder rattled and cracked round the horizon as he came out on to the quay. There were pleasure boats at the steps, unloading passengers, but no sign of the Wordens or of Helen. Feeling a little foolish he voiced his fears to one of the cap and jersey boys.

'You don't have to worry, me ol' dear, there's no wind behind this. The most they'll get is a wetting.'

The sea, in fact, was flat calm, ominously calm it seemed to him, and the colour of ink. A jagged lightning fork darted and branched several times over the outer harbour, followed at once by a ripping sound and the crash of another explosive thunderclap. The rain, which had been dripping half-heartedly, suddenly deluged down as though a great dam had burst, and everyone on the quay ran for cover. Wycliffe found himself wedged in the doorway of a café where the tables were already crowded with customers and the waitresses were rushed off their feet getting cups of tea and minerals.

The storm continued but during a lull in the rain Wycliffe slipped out, reached the main street and, keeping close to the shops, hurried along until he reached a flight of steps which provided a short-cut to his hotel.

Back in his room, he had a bath and changed his clothes. When he returned to his bedroom the rain was sheeting down once more, falling vertically and forming an impenetrable curtain which shut out the world. But the worst of the thunderstorm seemed to have passed, there were no more ear-splitting cracks overhead but a continuous clatter and rumble from further away. He was uneasy about Helen and Ruth but he had to admit that there had been scarcely a breath of wind.

He unlocked a suitcase, took out Gill's report and turned to the record of an interrogation of Terrence Rogers, book-keeper at the garage. It was so dark that he had to switch on the light.

Gill had noted by the man's name: 'Comes up to my shoulder and weighs 16 stone with egg on his tie.'

'What is your position here?'

'I keep the books. If this was a proper company I should be the secretary.'

'Is Cedric your boss?'

'Not if what I've heard about the will is right.'

'I should have said, *was* he your boss?'

'Nominally but not in fact. The old man owned the place and everybody knew it. If they didn't he soon put 'em right.'

'How did Cedric get on with his father?'

'You should ask him.'

'I'm asking you and as this is a murder investigation you would be well advised to answer.'

'O.K. Don't get steamed up. The answer to your question is that, for the most part, the old man pulled the strings and Ceddie danced.'

'For the most part, but sometimes he didn't, so what happened then?'

'Then there was trouble.' Wycliffe could imagine this remark accompanied by a fat chuckle.

'A row?'

'Not a row exactly because Ceddie never got a word in and the old man never raised his voice. He would just take Ceddie apart, chew up the bits and spit 'em out. I've had a grandstand seat more than once.'

'When was the last?'

'It must have been a fortnight before the old man got his ticket.'

'Here?'

'In this very office.'

'And you?'

'Me? I was out there with the blonde. I sent her off to powder her nose in case she heard things she shouldn't.'

'But you heard what it was about?'

'I didn't need to, I knew. You might say I started it. Cedric had been cooking the books and it wasn't the first time.'

'And you told his father?'

'I had to. It was bound to come out and it could easily have dropped me in the shit.'

'How much was involved?'

'Six fifty, give or take a fiver.'

'And the other times?'

'There was only one other time, at least since I've been here.'

'And how long is that?'

'Three years. He tried it on about six months back. It was so bloody clumsy I couldn't believe it was him and this time wasn't much better. Cedric is a bloody fool.'

'Did his father keep him short?'

'I'd like to be that short—you too, I reckon. He had a salary of two and a half thou' and fifty per cent of the net profit.'

'Amounting to . . . ?'

'In the average year he would gross seven thousand.'

'Enough to keep the wolf from the door.'

'And to pay for a bit of chicken on the side.'

'What does he do with it?'

'Search me! He's never been a miser; he drinks a fair bit and he has a flutter on the gee-gees but not more than he can afford. The old man bought the house for him. If you ask me, Ceddie's been in real trouble this past few months, he's gone down hill fast, but what it's all about I haven't a clue.'

'You're quite sure?'

'I've been frank, haven't I?'

'I hope so.'

'Do you think Ceddie really killed the old man?'

'What do you think?'

'Blowing the old boy up sticks in my gut. Christ, there must be easier ways... I mean, he could've gone out in the launch, pushed him overboard and as long as he came back wet nobody would ask too many questions.'

In his own unique way, the book-keeper was another member of the Cedric-couldn't-have-done-it club.

Wycliffe closed the file and put it away. He was thoughtful but he suffered from an inherent difficulty in putting his thoughts into words or, indeed, into a strictly logical sequence. His mind lacked precision; vague pictures, words and phrases, recollected sights, sounds and smells seemed to drift in and out of his consciousness as a substitute for true 'thought'. The same images turned up again and again in different associations, forming ever-changing patterns. He was rarely conscious of selecting one pattern rather than another but somehow, given time, a particular one would command his attention and then he would act. He had had the luck or the misfortune to be associated with several cases which had caught the attention of the news media and he had been interviewed many times on radio and television. When they asked him factual questions he gave factual answers but most other questions brought unhelpful replies. 'I don't know... I've no idea,' or even, just a shrug of the shoulders. So he had acquired a reputation for being both modest and shy.

Now he was acutely uneasy. He was not satisfied that Tremain had been murdered for his money. There was a theatrical aspect of the affair which worried him. What did he mean by theatrical? For once he would force himself to define his terms. A theatrical production is contrived, stage-managed. But so is any premeditated murder. Yes, but the primary object of theatre is to engage the emotions of an audience, not to achieve this or that end for a character portrayed on the stage. The player is a means not an end. He was pleased, so far. But what was he saying? That the old man's death had been contrived as a display? As an act? That would be nonsense, yet he felt that he was nibbling at the truth. He had pointed out to Franks that Tremain need not have been killed by the explosion, now he was saying that the old man's death was not *essential* to whatever plan had been made.

For the moment, he could go no further.

The rain had stopped and the air, washed clean, was astonishingly clear. The view from his window had the sharpness and definition as well as the sombre greyness of an etching. But the sky was definitely lightening. He decided that he would walk down to the quay again in the hope of meeting his wife and daughter.

He reached the quay just as they were climbing out of the dinghy, flushed and a little excited by their adventure.

'You should have seen the lightning on the sea, dad. Fantastic!'

It was rare for Ruth to let her enthusiasm for anything show itself. She was in a phase where such behaviour is 'gauche'. Helen took his warm hand in her cold one and whispered, 'Glad to be back.' But they were not even wet, they had crowded into the little cabin, leaving the crewman at the wheel.

After their evening meal Wycliffe asked his wife if she would like to go for a walk but Helen was tired and preferred to stay in the hotel lounge with a book. The storm had cleared the air, literally, and lowered the temperature so that the evening was chilly. The sky was a pale turquoise blue with massed black clouds on the horizon, edged with gold where they hid the sun.

Wycliffe gravitated, naturally, to the harbour and with as little thought entered the public bar of the Robartes Arms. For once, the bar was comfortably full and there was a hum of conversation. Walter Tyson was playing darts and there was a hand of whist in progress at one of the tables but the domino players were sitting, hands resting on thighs, watching the others. Wycliffe collected his drink and went over to them. Charlie Pullen moved up to make room.

'Sit down, sir. Plenty of room.'

'Quite a storm.'

Charlie nodded. 'All the better for it.'

From time to time Wycliffe was conscious of Tyson watching him as though he might be plucking up courage to come over and speak. When Wycliffe went to fetch drinks for himself and his immediate neighbours he passed close to Tyson and said, quietly, 'I would like a word—not here, afterwards.'

The darts match ended amid a good deal of noisy raillery and the losers went to the bar to stand their round.

Somebody, near Wycliffe, said, 'Geoff's late tonight,' and everyone in hearing laughed. For once, Charlie let him in on the joke.

'Over there, the little chap with the black hair. Table near the door . . . That's Geoff Williams, Eunice's husband. He's ten year younger than Eunice and a bit easy, if you understand me. She only lets him out for an hour a couple of times a week. You watch, he'll look up directly, see the time and he'll be through that door quicker than you could say knife.'

Sure enough, not many minutes had gone by before the little man glanced up at the clock, showed every sign of distress, gulped down his beer and dashed out. A gust of laughter followed him.

They sat in silence for a while, then Charlie Pullen said, abruptly, 'So they reckon young Cedric killed his father.'

Wycliffe was non-committal. 'Apparently.' It was obvious that the old man wanted to make a point and in order to do so he had been forced to open a conversation with a comparative stranger.

'I don't go along with that myself.' Charlie took an extravagant gulp from his tankard. 'Not the way it was done.' He wiped his mouth with the back of his hand. 'Cedric might have killed his father or anybody else in a fit of temper but not in cold blood, not thinking about it, working it out then doing it. It's not in the nature of the man.'

'That's up to the jury to decide now.'

'Maybe, but juries have been wrong before.'

It was almost as though there had been a conspiracy. But if they were right? Somebody had murdered Harry Tremain and that somebody must fulfil certain rather stringent conditions. He had broken into the explosives store at the quarry; he knew how to use the explosives he stole to make a species of time-bomb. He had access to *Green Lady IV* (not very difficult) and presumably he had a reason for murdering Harry Tremain or, at least, for endangering his life. This hypothetical person had also done his best—his successful best—to incriminate Cedric. Surely the number of people who met such specifications must be very small? Indeed, could there be such a person? Was it not more reasonable to believe that Cedric had killed his father for his money?

Wycliffe stayed long enough to buy another round then he left.

Outside it was dusk, the tide had turned and was lifting the craft in the basin on to even keels, their masts level with the quay. The navigation lights were lit and there were lights in many of the houses. Wycliffe lingered by the quay rail outside the pub and, after a moment or two, what he was expecting happened. Walter Tyson came out and looked up and down the quay. When he caught sight of Wycliffe he hesitated, then came over.

'Mr Tyson, isn't it?'

'You're a detective, aren't you? You wanted to speak to me?'

Wycliffe tried to put him at his ease. 'As a matter of fact, I came here on holiday.'

A forced laugh which made a curious whistling sound in his deformed nostrils. 'I came here more than two years ago for a holiday and I'm still here.' His speech was rather slow because of difficulty in enunciation and his voice was expressionless, as with a person who has been born deaf.

'You work on the caravan site, don't you?'

'I run it. The books and all the organization.'

Wycliffe had started to walk away from the pub along the quay and Tyson fell into step beside him. He was half a head taller than Wycliffe but his stride was short so that he walked in a stilted fashion, almost a mincing gait. No doubt his legs had been injured also.

'It was about the caravan site I wanted to talk to you. I believe a Miss Ritter rents a van there?'

'She rents one of our permanent stands.'

'How long has she been on the site?'

'About eight months, she came at the beginning of the winter.'

'A nice woman?'

Tyson took his time. 'Not exactly the type I like to have in the permanents, I prefer families, but she pays her rent. I'm not one to look for scandal but a man visits her from time to time and sometimes he stays for two or three days. She says that he is her brother and, of course, he may be . . .'

'What does she do for a living?'

Tyson shrugged. 'That's one of the things which bothers me, she doesn't seem to do anything.'

'This man, what is he like?'

'Tall, my age or a bit older, well dressed . . .'

'But?'

'I think he's seen better days. He struck me as having gone to seed a bit.'

Which might add up to Dandy Wilson.

They had reached the top of the slipway where *Green Lady IV* stood on her cradle, the painted name-board on her stern just visible in the fading light.

'Unusual colour for a fishing boat,' Wycliffe said. He had the impression that Tyson had more to say and that he needed encouragement.

The nervous, whistling laugh. 'It's a tradition, the Tremain boats have always been that colour.'

'I believe that you were a friend of Harry's?'

'Not a friend, exactly. Harry wasn't a man to make friends but I used to go out crabbing with him in the winter when I hadn't much to do.'

The quays were almost deserted and it was dark enough for the harbour lights to send a shimmering yellow path across the water. Wycliffe did not speak and Tyson went on:

'I suppose you know that he was a wealthy man?'

'I know that he was well off.'

Tyson was silent for a while. 'It didn't do him much good. Several times he's said to me, "It's not very pleasant, Walter, when all your family want from you is your money", or words to that effect.'

'He said that?'

'More than once. And on one occasion he added, "Sometimes I wonder whether that boy of mine can wait." '

There was silence between them for some time then Tyson said, 'Mr Wycliffe . . .'

'Yes?'

'Are you re-opening the case? I mean, is Cedric going to be released?'

Wycliffe was brusque. 'Tremain has been charged and committed.'

Tyson was startled by the change in the chief superintendent's manner. He murmured something and made off up the narrow alley which led to the square. Wycliffe stood for a while beside *Green Lady IV*, smoking his pipe and waiting for Tyson's footsteps to die away. Tyson had disturbed him and he could not understand why. Was it because of the effort which speech cost him that he had seemed so intense?

He tapped out his pipe and walked slowly back to the hotel without meeting a soul. Williams, the little old man who served as porter and general dogsbody at the hotel, was in reception. He looked at Wycliffe over his spectacles and asked him to wait.

'Madam would like a word, sir.'

He mumbled something into the house telephone and a minute or so later the proprietress arrived wearing an evening gown which draped yards of blue, filmy material over her tiny frame. She gave Wycliffe a twisted smile and glided behind the counter as though propelled on wheels.

'I've got something for you, chief superintendent.'

She unlocked an old-fashioned safe and produced a large, buff envelope.

'A policeman brought this for you and I thought that I had better put it into a place of safe keeping.'

Wycliffe took the envelope, thanked her and wished her good-night. Bourne must have sent the twenty-year-old file by special messenger after all.

He went up to his room where Helen was getting ready for bed but he did not feel in the least tired himself. To be honest, the newly arrived file tempted him like the next chapter of an absorbing novel.

'Going out tomorrow?'

'No, the Wordens are having a day shopping.'

There was a pause while Helen applied cleansing cream round her eyes.

'Charles . . .'

'Yes?'

'I think they're cooling off.'

'Who is cooling off?'

'Ruth and young Worden.'

'Good.'

'Don't be like that, the Wordens are very pleasant people and Ruth could do a lot worse for herself.'

'I don't doubt it but they're not our sort.'

He knew from the smile she gave him that they were at one again.

'Anyway, Ruth is coming here tomorrow while they go shopping so if you have things to do you don't have to bother with me.'

He changed into a dressing-gown and picked up the envelope. 'I'd like to have a look at this before I come to bed. Shall I disturb you if I sit here by the window? The bedside lamp . . .'

'My dear Charles, I don't think a brass band would keep me awake tonight.'

He sat in a wicker chair which was designed to creak with every slightest movement and when he had been turning the pages for some time Helen said, sleepily, 'To be honest, I'm rather glad too.'

It was a bulky file and he turned the pages, idly at first, until he became absorbed. Out of the terse official reports, first of police interrogations and statements then of committal proceedings and of the trial, there emerged a story which took him back twenty years in the life of the village he was coming to know. As he read, it seemed to him that the endless battalions of trippers melted away with the ice-cream stalls, the cafés and the gift shops, revealing a simpler, more fundamental pattern of life in which the whole village reacted more as a family reacts to the fortunes and foibles of its members.

Chapter Nine

'WHEN WAS THE last time you went out with Alice Weekes?'

'On Tuesday evening.'

'Were you in love with her?'

'I thought I was.'

And there were questions about Eunice:

'Did you have intercourse with your cousin?'

'No.'

'But you have stated that you purchased contraceptives to that end.'

'I tried to.'

'You mean that you tried to have intercourse with her?'

'Yes.'

'But she would not allow it, is that what you are trying to tell me?'

'No, she wanted it but I couldn't . . .'

The character of this young man, Morley Tremain, was beginning to emerge. Sensitive, introspective, dominated by a managing and possessive mother. Fatherless.

'Have you ever seen a girl who has been raped and strangled?'

'Are you telling me that Alice is dead?'

'We found her this morning.'

'She had been raped?'

'Yes.'

It was like looking through the wrong end of a telescope. It had all happened in 1953 while the Christie trial was still holding the headlines, headlines only recently taken over from the Coronation. Wycliffe had been a detective sergeant then and he had never heard of the Tremain case.

Prosecuting Counsel to a witness:

'Did you see someone running towards you from the direction of the old engine-house?'

'I did.'

'Did you recognize that person?'

'As he came nearer, it was Morley Tremain, the accused.'

And Morley's statement:

'When I reached the engine-house I walked round the back and looked inside where there is a square of grass almost enclosed by the ruin. I do not know what made me do this. On the grass, behind a mound of rubble, I saw the body of Alice Weekes. She was partially undressed, her clothes were torn and she lay on her back with her legs apart. Her face was distorted and discoloured. I was very frightened and I think I ran away from the place.'

Harry Tremain, the boy's uncle, now murdered himself:

'I was at the window, focusing my glasses on objects at different distances when I noticed people on the top path...' (Wycliffe had been in that room and stood looking out of that same window. The old man's glasses were still there, after twenty years.)

'Did you recognize them?'

'I saw that one of them was my nephew and the other was Alice Weekes.'

'The prisoner and the murdered girl?'

'Yes, sir.'

'Were you surprised to see your nephew with Alice Weekes?'

'Yes, I was.'

'Why?'

'Because I thought that was all over...'

'Did you mention what you had seen to any member of your family or to anyone else?'

'Yes, I did. When I went downstairs, I said to my wife that I had seen Morley on the top path with Alice Weekes.'

'Was anyone else there when you told your wife what you had seen?'

'Yes, sir. My son, my daughter Eunice, and my grandfather. My grandfather is ninety-eight and he wouldn't have heard me or wouldn't have understood if he had.'

Helen turned over in her sleep with a little moan of contentment. The curtains did not quite meet and through the gap he could see the sea bathed in moonlight. From his early days as a beat copper he had always felt at his best in the small hours, relaxed and at peace with himself. For a while the pressure seems to be off, one can live at one's own pace and still feel secure. Perhaps because those who might threaten or betray or undermine are asleep? Automatically he reached for his pipe and lit it, although he made a general rule not to smoke in the bedroom.

He was nearing the end of the file, he had skimmed a lot, much he had read in detail. He would need to spend more time but an idea was emerging, an idea which, ironically, received another breath of support from the closing speech for the Crown:

'. . . I come now to the assertion by the accused in one of his several statements to the effect that he saw his cousin, Cedric Tremain, running down the slope to his house. I am sure that the implication of this convenient recollection did not escape you. The prosecution does not have to answer random, unsupported statements of this kind but, nevertheless, you will have noted that it was the unanimous testimony of Cedric Tremain's father, mother and sister, that he did not leave the house that afternoon. He was, in fact, confined to his bed with a severe bilious attack brought on by something he had eaten.'

And before the judge passed sentence the Clerk of the Court asked:

'Prisoner at the Bar, you stand convicted of murder, have

you anything to say before judgement of death is passed according to law?'

'I am not guilty, I did not kill her!'

Morley Tremain was sentenced to death. The record went on to show that he had appealed and that his appeal had been rejected, his sentence was, however, commuted by the Home Secretary, to life imprisonment.

Morley Tremain served fourteen years of his sentence and, on his release, went to live with his mother in Southampton, where she had lived throughout the fourteen years and visited him regularly in prison.

Bourne had done his best in a short time to bring the file up to date.

Morley had lived quietly with his mother for three years, during which time he worked in the assembly shop of a firm which marketed accounting machines and calculators. Then Sarah Tremain died. Morley, released from parole, sold his mother's furniture and left their rented house. The police had no reason to take any further interest in him and nothing more was known. But Wycliffe was able to add the information he had gathered in the village, that Morley had met his death in a road accident.

He closed the file, tapped out his pipe and went to bed but he did not get to sleep at once, his mind was too active. Oddly enough he was not thinking about the twenty-year-old case but about Cedric Tremain and his present plight.

Gill had been convinced that Cedric was being blackmailed and there was good evidence to support the idea. Over the past six months he had withdrawn substantial sums from his bank and his account was now overdrawn. He had tried to obtain credit on his expectations and even to mortgage the house although his father held the deeds. And one must add the two feeble attempts to defraud his father. But, despite sustained pressure, Cedric would not admit to being blackmailed and he explained his financial straits by saying that he had been gambling heavily. For which, incidentally, there was no evidence.

Faced with this refusal and with the fact that he could find no likely grounds for blackmail, Gill had given up that line of enquiry. It was not vital to his case; it was enough that Cedric had been desperately short of money for whatever reason. All the same . . .

Was there a link with the twenty-year-old crime?

A young man, green and tender as a spring shoot, aping his less scrupulous and worldly-wise cousin, had blundered into sex and made a hash of it. He had been convicted of murder in the act of rape and spent fourteen years in gaol. Twenty years after his crime his uncle was murdered and his cousin charged with killing him. Coincidence? Possibly; but Wycliffe's experience had taught him to be wary of coincidence. He was much more inclined to see the events as part of a pattern. Like a good Confucianist he was convinced of a symmetry in human affairs, he believed that events are balanced one against another, that every action produces its ultimate and inevitable reaction.

As his eyes began to stay closed of their own accord and his thoughts became deliciously vague, he seemed to see that pattern. He was looking down on it as though it were indeed a geometrical design, a true tapestry of events. He must remember . . . must remember . . .

The next time he opened his eyes it was broad daylight and the sun was shining. He turned over to see the time by the clock on his bedside table and caught sight of the file. What was it that he had been so anxious to remember? Whatever it was escaped him now.

Ten minutes to seven.

'Are you awake?' Helen, sleepily.

'Yes.'

'How do you feel?'

'All right. Shouldn't I?'

'Well, you are convalescing.'

He had forgotten.

They had breakfast together in the dining-room overlooking the bay. The hotel was full but there were few guests breakfasting so early: a young woman with fair hair and blue eyes and two little girls, twins, who would grow up exactly like her; two middle-aged couples like themselves and a solitary lady who sat bolt upright looking neither to her right nor her left. Ruth arrived when they had reached their second cup of coffee and the room was beginning to fill. She was brown as a hazel nut and her hair had bleached in the sun and wind. As she came into the dining-room Wycliffe saw her, for once, as a stranger and he was aware that the eyes of other men in the room were on her. She seemed pleased to be with them and he was moved by her affection but for some reason which he could not have explained his response was gruff.

'Well, I've got work to do.'

'*Work?* I thought you were convalescing.'

A look from her mother made her drop the subject.

He had decided to go to the caravan site to talk to Elaine Ritter and, because he was on holiday, he decided to walk. After all, his time was his own. It was a fine morning but a freshness in the air and puffy white clouds which sometimes obscured the sun warned that the spell of settled weather had ended with the storm.

Did Cedric Tremain kill his father? For two days the question had been in his mind, irritating like the absurd refrain of a catchy tune. Now there was another question arising from the report of the twenty-year old murder: Did Morley Tremain kill Alice Weekes?

A fanciful idea had taken root in his mind which refused to yield to logic or common sense. The evidence strongly suggested that, despite his denials, Cedric had been blackmailed. On what grounds? Gill had failed to answer that question. Wyclife's idea was that if Cedric and not Morley had been guilty of the girl's murder the fact would still be a powerful blackmail weapon. But in whose hands? Obviously someone who knew the truth and could prove it. But if there was such a person why had he or she waited twenty years before doing something about it? In any case it was absurd to suppose that Cedric would have raped a girl who had gone with him willingly enough a few days before.

Wycliffe muttered irritably as he climbed the hill out of the village.

Before he reached the line of elms bordering the site he was reminded again that he had been ill, this time by his pounding heart. But he had done better than at any other time so far. Anyway, his depression had vanished.

There was one residential caravan on a concrete standing just inside the entrance, presumably Tyson's. There was nobody in the little glass-fronted office but the barrier was raised. There was a queue at the camp shop for newspapers and milk; people were carrying buckets and plastic water containers to and from the standpipes and children were playing on the cinder paths because the grass was still too wet after the storm.

The permanent stands were at the end of the main roadway, a dozen so-called mobile homes each with its little patch of fenced-off garden. The curtains were drawn at number eight and when Wycliffe knocked a woman with her hair in curlers put her head out of the window of the next van.

'They're not up yet.'

He knocked again, more insistently and after a while he heard someone moving about inside. The door opened outwards and he had to stand aside. A woman in a floral wrap looked at him sleepily.

'What do you want?'

She was much younger than he had expected, perhaps twenty-eight or nine, plump but not fat, and pretty in a fluffy-blonde way. She had make-up on from the previous day. She tried half-heartedly to suppress a yawn.

Wycliffe showed her his warrant card and she made a resigned grimace. 'You'd better come in.'

The door opened into the living-room which was untidy and squalid. Crumbs and cigarette ash had been walked into the carpet, dirty china, glasses and bottles littered the table and overflowed on to the floor. She removed newspapers from one of the chairs and invited him to sit down. The room stank of stale beer and cigarette smoke.

'Sorry, it's a bit of a mess but I had some friends in last night.' She reached for a packet of cigarettes and lit one, drawing deeply, then coughing. 'What do you want? I suppose it's the old man?'

'You are a friend of Cedric Tremain?'

She sighed. 'Here we go again.' She blew smoke through cupid's-bow lips. 'Yes, you could say that we were friendly.'

The wrap she was wearing kept falling open and she wore nothing underneath.

'You occasionally spent the night with him?'

'Is that illegal?'

'When were you last there?'

'Last Sunday week. Look, they had me down to the temporary nick on the quay and I made a statement. It's all there.'

'I know, I've read it.'

'Well?'

'According to your statement you spent the whole of Sunday night with Cedric.'

'So I did.'

'And you are prepared to say that in court?'

'If I have to.'

She was on edge. The door which led, presumably, into the bedroom was a little ajar and she got up to close it.

'So you can tell me what he was like. Was he tense? Keyed up? Or was he much as usual?'

She was not very bright but she sensed danger in the question and hesitated. Eeny, meeny, miney, mo . . .

'He seemed like usual.'

Wycliffe was bland. 'That surprises me in a man who had just arranged to murder his own father.'

She pounced. 'That's where you're wrong. Cedric didn't kill the old man.'

'I was going to say *or* a man who was being blackmailed as he certainly was.'

That shot went home. 'Blackmailed?' For a moment she was too shaken to do more than sit, looking blank.

Wycliffe got out his pipe and seemed about to light it when he stood up quickly. 'I think it's time we had your friend in.' He threw open the door which she had closed, to disclose Dandy Wilson on the other side. Evidently he had been listening and he was only half dressed, in trousers and vest.

'Come in, Dandy. I thought it might be you. On vacation?'

Wilson came in, looking absurdly sheepish. 'Good morning, Mr Wycliffe, what's going on?'

Dandy was certainly going to seed; his face was flabby, his eyes and mouth moist and his expression lugubrious, so that Wycliffe half expected his features to crease like that of some fat, petulant baby and to dissolve into tears. If women still fell for him, as they appeared to do, it must be because his damp vulnerability rekindled the maternal flame.

'A bit off your beat, aren't you, Dandy?'

'As you said yourself, Mr Wycliffe, I'm on holiday.'

Elaine had started to pick up the glasses and bottles and to stack them on the table.

'Combining business with pleasure.'

Dandy lowered himself into an easy chair. 'You'll have to explain that, Mr Wycliffe.'

'Gladly.' Wycliffe had decided on the line he would take; it was a fishing expedition and the catch was unpredictable. 'The police case against Cedric Tremain is that he murdered his father because he was desperately in need of money.'

Dandy looked only politely interested. 'I see.'

'And he was short of money because he was being blackmailed.'

Dandy was massaging one side of his protuberant paunch. 'You must excuse me, Mr Wycliffe, but I'm not well this morning. Something I ate.'

'Or drank.' Elaine had given up her perfunctory attempt to tidy the room and was standing, absentmindedly, scratching her breast under her wrap.

Despite his many convictions Dandy was no fool. 'I've never blackmailed anybody, Mr Wycliffe, never.'

Wycliffe was smooth. 'More accurately, you've never been sent down for blackmail but you've come pretty near it more than once.'

'I don't know what you're talking about, Mr Wycliffe.'

'Get dressed, Wilson.'

He looked surprised and aggrieved. 'Are you taking me in, Mr Wycliffe? What for? What have I done?'

Wycliffe rarely raised his voice or even spoke with any special emphasis and he did not do so now. His manner was relaxed and conversational, his face devoid of expression.

'I'm taking you both in for questioning on suspicion of being concerned in the murder of Harry Tremain.'

Wilson was rattled and he was pale. 'Concerned in ... I've never met either of the Tremains, father or son. You've got nothing on me this time, Mr Wycliffe, nothing.'

'You think not? You've moved out of your class, Dandy, and you know how dangerous that is. This latest little exercise has driven a man to murder and you are accessories—both of you.'

'You'll have a job to prove that, Mr Wycliffe.'

Wycliffe tapped his pipe out into an ashtray. 'No problem. In a case like this we shall take you apart. We haven't always got the time to waste on small-time crooks but when it comes to murder—'

'But you've no evidence, Mr Wycliffe. I've been going straight.' Dandy was looking ludicrously woebegone and the girl was standing with her mouth open as though she had intended to say something but had forgotten what it was.

'With the money that's passed through your hands over the past six months, Dandy, do you think we'll have trouble finding evidence? In any case, how long do you think Elaine, here, would stand up to real questioning—or you either, for that matter? By the way, I thought I told you to get dressed.'

But Wilson did not move, he was working things out before committing himself. 'You are threatening me, Mr Wycliffe.'

'So?'

'You are not one to threaten unless you want something, am I

141

right?' Dandy was earnest, like a schoolboy trying to get his lesson right.

'Very likely.'

'And if I co-operate?'

'No deals, Dandy.'

'What do you want to know, Mr Wycliffe?'

'That's simple. Who gave you the dirt on Cedric Tremain?'

Wilson looked surprised. 'The straight answer to that is that I haven't got anything on him, nothing.'

'I don't call that co-operation.'

'But it's the truth, Mr Wycliffe.' His eyes were anxious. He hesitated for a while then added, on a harder note, 'I think I ought to know what I'm letting myself in for.'

'You'll have to take a chance.'

Wilson sighed. 'Tremain *thought* I had something on him, that's the truth.'

'And what gave him that idea, a bad dream?'

Wilson reached for a cigarette, put it into a long holder and lit it. 'I'll tell you, Mr Wycliffe. Just over six months ago I was staying here with Elaine as I am now and I had a letter, an anonymous letter—'

'Who knew you were here?'

Wilson was reflective. 'It's hard to say, I—'

'Never mind. What did the letter say?'

'Just this: "If you want to supplement your income try telling Cedric that you are in possession of information about a terrible crime which would interest the police." '

'You have this letter?'

'What do you think I am, Mr Wycliffe? I burned it.'

For once, Wycliffe believed him.

'Does Cedric know that it was you—?'

'Certainly not.'

What Wilson had told him, improbable as it might sound, was very likely true. Dandy would have found it impossible to resist such a bait dangled in that particular way. He would have risen to it like a trout to a well-chosen fly. Whoever had sent him

142

that anonymous letter must have known him well. But who would want to do Dandy a good turn, or more likely, Cedric an ill one? Cedric had paid to the limit; if Gill was right, beyond the limit. So Cedric had a massive load on his conscience and somebody who knew about it was using that knowledge to break him.

Wycliffe had not spoken for some time and Dandy and the girl were watching him as though he were some awe-inspiring oracle. Outside, children were playing on the cinder path, kicking a ball which, now and then, struck the side of the van with a resounding thud. At last, Dandy could stand the suspense no longer.

'What more do you want from me, Mr Wycliffe?'

Wycliffe looked at him as though mildly surprised by the interruption. 'What? Oh, nothing more at the moment.' He got up and stood, staring down at Dandy who almost cowered in his chair. 'I hope, for your sake, that you've told me the truth, Dandy.'

'I have, Mr Wycliffe.'

'And you've no idea who it was that put you on to Cedric Tremain?'

'None, Mr Wycliffe. I swear.'

Wycliffe shrugged and turned to the outside door which he opened, revealing a rectangle of almost blinding light.

'You've been very decent, Mr Wycliffe.'

'Not really, Dandy. If Cedric Tremain could be persuaded to admit that he was being blackmailed your holiday wouldn't last long.'

If anything the weather was pleasanter than it had been, fresher and not so oppressively hot. A car towing a caravan and two others with tents stored on their roof-racks were waiting by Reception. Tyson, in his little glass office, was dealing with the owner of the caravan. He saw Wycliffe and it was obvious that he would have liked to speak, but he could not keep his customers waiting and Wycliffe walked on with only a casual wave of the hand.

'. . . a terrible crime which would interest the police.' 'A terrible crime,' the phrase, somehow, seemed oddly chosen. A moment's thought and he realized why. It was an emotive phrase, unlikely to have been used in the circumstances unless the writer was personally involved, a victim, directly or indirectly, of the crime. In any case, what he had discovered in no way weakened Gill's case against Cedric, rather it was strengthened by the filling in of additional detail. But Wycliffe felt dissatisfied, although he could not have explained why.

On his way back to the village he had to join the crowds trooping down from the car and coach parks. Many of the children were carrying buckets and spades, though there was no beach.

Someone had induced Wilson to blackmail Cedric without profit to himself. Surely this must mean that the someone had a bitter grievance against Cedric? As a result of the blackmail pressure Cedric murdered his father by means of an explosive device which, to say the least, was an unreliable weapon. His thoughts reverted to the possibility that Cedric might have been guilty of the earlier crime.

'It doesn't make sense.'

Wycliffe had spoken the words aloud to himself and drew curious glances from at least two of the passers-by.

Thirty years ago Sidney Tremain had hanged himself, ten years later his son was sentenced for the murder of his girl-friend, now Sidney's brother, Harry, is murdered and Harry's son is charged with the crime. A pattern of violence . . . A pattern? Or unrelated events?

Wycliffe worked his way through the narrow main street where a harassed traffic warden was in altercation with the driver of a large van. He took the short-cut, up the steps, to his hotel. There was nobody in Reception and he went up to his room where one of the maids was making the bed. She was a woman in her sixties, small, wrinkled, probably a widow or a spinster, at any rate, the victim of a hard life.

'I suppose you've lived in the village a long time?'

'All my life.'

'You must know the Tremain family pretty well.'

She twisted the wedding ring on her finger. (Widow, not

spinster.) 'Pretty well. I went to school with Harry and with his brother, Sidney, the one that hung himself. I could have married Harry if I'd a mind to.' She stood, smoothing her black apron, waiting.

It was tantalizing. This woman and, probably, a score of others in the village, knew the Tremains better than he could ever hope to know them. Their knowledge might, indirectly, have provided the solutions to his problems but what questions should he ask when he had no idea what it was that he wanted to know?

'Did Harry Tremain's wife come from the village?'

'No, she was one of the Treneer girls from over to Penhallick. I never had no great opinion of Clara nor she of me. All tarred with the same brush, they Treneers was. Mean! They wouldn't give anybody the time of day.' She pursed her thin lips. 'Look how she treated her half-sister.'

'Her half-sister?'

'Ella Jordan. Ella was a daughter to Clara's mother by her first husband and she come to live with Clara after Eunice was born. Made a proper slave of her Clara did; treated her like a servant—worse. O' course, she was a Catholic.'

'That made a difference?'

'It did in they days. The village was all chapel and the Tremains most of anybody. Now nobody takes no notice of that sort of thing but they did then. Ella had a hard life.' She fingered her little snub nose. 'In the end she come into a bit of money and it was just as well for her, poor toad.'

'When did she come into this money?'

'When? How should I know? I remember it was after the war, a good bit after.'

'After or before the time when Alice Weekes was murdered?'

'After, but not long after—'

'She left The Quay House?'

'She'd have bin a fool if she didn't. I heard she bought a little house somewhere but it didn't interest me.'

'But she was living at The Quay House at the time of the murder—you are sure of that?'

'O' course I'm sure. I aren't gone soft in the head yet.'

'Where is she now?'

'Dead and gone I should think, she must be an old woman if she's still above ground.'

'Thank you for talking to me.'

'You're welcome.'

When she had gone Wycliffe got out the file of the earlier case and turned the pages, dipping here and there.

'Was there anyone else there when you told your wife what you had seen?'

'Yes, sir. My son, my daughter Eunice, and my grandfather. My grandfather is ninety-eight and he wouldn't have heard or he wouldn't have understood if he had.'

He leafed through the file from beginning to end. It seemed that there was no mention of Ella Jordan, no statement had been taken from her, neither did she appear as a witness at the trial. It probably meant nothing but it was odd that someone who lived at The Quay House should not have been mentioned.

He picked up the telephone and had to wait a little while before he heard the proprietress's tight little voice.

'Can I help you?'

He gave the number of Southampton CID. Without knowing why, he had decided to keep the investigation in his own hands. Officially, so far, there was no investigation and he hoped that he could keep it that way.

When he had been put through he asked to speak to Chief Inspector Chubb, a former colleague who had worked under him as a sergeant. They greeted each other and chatted for a few moments nostalgically.

'Tremain? I'll certainly look into it ... A road accident ... Released in '67. Three years living with his mother brings us up to '70. It shouldn't be difficult to find the address if she lived there for seventeen years ... I'll follow it up and ring you when

I've got something . . . Think nothing of it, Mr Wycliffe. I owe you, if you remember . . .'

It was only as he was going out that he noticed an envelope propped against the mirror of the dressing-table. It was addressed to him in his daughter's writing:

Mum's gone shopping with me, be home sixish so make the most of it,

Love R.

Why did the note make him feel a little sad?

Chapter Ten

INEVITABLY HE WAS back on the quay by lunch-time, having a drink in the public bar. Tyson was there and Wycliffe was fully expecting the man to approach him but Tyson contented himself with a nod and continued playing darts. Wycliffe joined his friends the domino players.

The sky had clouded over and there were occasional flurries of rain so that there were few tourists or trippers about. Like flies, they swarm in the sunshine and, as with flies, it is a mystery what happens to them when it is dull or raining. He had not booked a table but shortly before one o'clock the barman came over.

'Your table is ready, sir, if you would like to go through.'

The doctor seemed to be enjoying a small joke at his expense. They ordered beef with a bottle of claret.

'Not made up your mind yet?'

Wycliffe ignored the question. 'I don't think I'll take the soup.'

After the main course had been served Wycliffe said, 'Where is the nearest Roman Catholic priest?'

Langley looked surprised. 'There's one in town, Father Nesbitt, a real chip off the old Jesuit block. I meet him occasionally, we are both on the governing body of a school for handicapped children.'

'Do you remember Ella Jordan?'

The doctor screwed up his lips. 'Can't say I do.'

'She lived at The Quay House, she was a half-sister to Harry Tremain's wife; a sort of slavey for the family, poor relation.'

'I do remember they had somebody there but I can't say that I ever met her.'

After lunch Wycliffe walked along the quay to the slate-fronted house. The showers had passed and a watery sun was struggling through the clouds. The door was open but there was no sign of the cat. He knocked and his knock was answered by the little man he had seen in the pub—Geoff. He was youngish but wrinkled and swarthy, his chin sprouted dark bristles.

'Mr Williams?'

Wycliffe introduced himself. The little man looked at him with lugubrious concern. 'You want to see my wife?'

'You are a laboratory assistant at the technical college, is that right, Mr Williams?'

'That's right, but I don't see—'

'Which department?'

'Biology, I look after the animals.'

Guinea-pigs, no doubt. Mr Williams looked like a sad, harmless little rodent, anxious to scamper away at the first opportunity.

'I'll fetch the wife.'

Wycliffe felt sure that Williams had never murdered anybody.

He left Wycliffe at the door and went back to the kitchen. Eunice did not come at once and when she did she looked flustered.

'You'd better come in here.'

'I'd rather go to your father's room.'

'Suit yourself, but what you expect to find up there I can't imagine.' She was angry and Wycliffe suspected that she had been venting her anger on her husband.

On the stairs she threw over her shoulder, 'I've been to see my lawyer. I'm going to contest the will.'

Wycliffe said nothing.

'What do they think we're going to live on? What good is this house with nothing to keep it up? It's monstrous!' She paused as they reached the top of the stairs and turned to face him. 'You know how she did it as well as I do. You've seen her. She's a whore, that's what she is. She used to come here to see him half-naked, see-through blouse, showing everything and he was fool enough . . .' She searched Wycliffe's face for some sign of response and finding none turned her venom on him. 'Men!

149

You're all the same, only one thing you think about when it comes down to it. Disgusting!'

The door of the old man's room was open and she led the way. 'Well, there you are, make the most of it.'

The room was as he had seen it before but he was seeing it with new eyes.

'Was this your parents' room before your mother died?'

She seemed surprised by the question. 'It's the best room in the house and look at it.'

'On Sunday 28th June, at approximately 2 p.m. were you in one of the bedrooms of your house?'

'I was.'

'What were you doing there?'

'I was cleaning my binoculars.'

'In the bedroom?'

'When I'm not using them I keep them on the chest-of-drawers.'

'After you had cleaned them did you try them out?'

'I did.'

'Tell the Court what you did and what you saw.'

'I was at the window focusing my glasses on objects at different distances when I noticed people on the top path.'

. . .'Did you recognize them?'

'I saw that one of them was my nephew and the other was Alice Weekes.'

'The prisoner and the murdered girl?'

'Yes, sir.'

Wycliffe picked up the binoculars from the chest-of-drawers and walked over to the window which looked out over the harbour and cliffs. He focused on the cliff path where, despite the uncertain weather, a trickle of people made their way to Wicca Cove, some of them carrying picnic baskets. He raised the glasses, sweeping the steep slopes covered with gorse and heather, to near the sky-line where a line of gorse bushes probably marked the top path. Away to the left the jagged stump of a mine chimney stabbed upwards against the sky.

'There is nobody on the top path today.'

'The top path?' The strain in her voice was unmistakable.

'Isn't that what they call the old path which runs through to the mine-workings?' He was still looking through the binoculars.

'There's no path there now, it's grown over.'

'But that was where your father saw your cousin and Alice Weekes on the afternoon she was murdered?'

There was silence for long enough to raise the tension. They could both hear the gulls crying outside and the putt-putt of one of the little self-drive motor boats. Then she said in a low voice, 'Why bring that up? It happened more than twenty years ago and it's all over now.'

He turned from the window to face her. She was moving round the room, straightening this, shifting that, picking things up and putting them down again.

'Your father said at the trial that he had seen them through his glasses from his window. Afterwards he went downstairs to the kitchen and mentioned what he had seen. Were you there to hear what your father said?'

'Yes, I was washing the dinner dishes.' Her voice was barely audible. She stood still now, her hands limply at her sides and he could see the blood pulsing through the translucent skin of her temples.

'You have an excellent memory.'

'You don't forget things like that.'

'Who else was there?'

'Mother and great-grandfather Tremain.'

'Cedric?'

An appreciable pause. 'No.'

'Where was Cedric?'

Her eyes behind the large circular lenses were focused on his face, unblinking. 'He was in bed, ill, he had a bilious attack.'

Wycliffe nodded as though satisfied. 'That is what he said at the trial and you supported him. It is also what your father said in his statement to the police.'

'Well?'

'It is not what your father said in answer to a question at the trial. It seems that nobody noticed the discrepancy, but it was there. At the trial your father, when asked who was in the kitchen apart from your mother, said, "My son, my daughter Eunice, and my grandfather . . ." '

'He must have made a slip, he was nervous, we all were.'

'What about Ella Jordan?'

'She was my mother's half-sister.'

'I know, but was she in the kitchen when your father came downstairs?'

'No, I don't think she was.'

'What happened to her?'

'What do you mean, what happened to her?'

'Where is she now?'

'I think she died. I fancy father mentioned it.'

'You don't know for certain?'

'No. She came into a bit of money and she left. She was a Catholic.'

'When did she leave?'

'It must have been nearly twenty years ago.'

'Not long after the murder?'

'I suppose not. I've never thought about it.'

Wycliffe had moved over to the roll-topped desk and opened one of the drawers.

'You don't mind?'

She made some vague gesture.

He took out the manilla envelope of photographs, slipped them on to the desk and started to shuffle through them. When he came to the studio portrait of the thin young man with weak eyes he held it up.

'Your cousin, the one who was sentenced to death for murder.'

She nodded. 'They didn't hang him, I told you—'

'No, he got life imprisonment. How long did he serve?'

She found it difficult to control her voice. 'Fourteen years.'

Wycliffe, the photograph in his hand, went to stand within a couple of feet of her. She moved so that there was a kitchen chair between them and she gripped the back as though for support. He could see little beads of sweat on her forehead.

'He served fourteen years,' Wycliffe repeated. 'You heard when he was released?'

'Yes.'

'How did you hear?'

She hesitated. 'I telephoned the prison at about the time I thought he was due to come out but he had already been released.'

'Had you contacted the prison before?'

She was thinking carefully before answering each question. 'Once or twice.'

'In other words you kept yourself informed about him.'

'I suppose so.'

'Why?'

'I wanted to know. Surely it's natural.'

'Because you were afraid?'

'Why should I be afraid?'

He was standing very close to her, staring into her eyes. 'You are afraid now.'

She endured his gaze as long as she could then found release in anger. 'This is absurd! All because my father made a slip in giving evidence twenty years ago. I thought it was your job to find out who killed him. You evidently don't think it was Cedric, otherwise you wouldn't be here now.'

Wycliffe cut in quietly. 'Your father's evidence at the trial may well have been a slip of the tongue, as you say, but it made me look at the two cases in a new light. That is what has brought me here now.'

She was silent, standing, gripping the chair, whiter than seemed possible. Wycliffe was afraid that she would faint. He turned away, to the other window this time. The sun had come out and in the basin some children were trying to set a blue sail on a varnished dinghy. The two boys were getting in each other's way while a golden-haired girl watched, serenely, from the stern. All three wore orange life-jackets. The cheerful, colourful scene was in poignant contrast with the tired, grey pattern of life in the slate house.

'I've been reading the police transcripts of evidence.' He spoke, still with his back to her. 'It seems that you wanted to marry your cousin; why didn't you?'

The silence lasted so long that he had given up expecting a reply but at last the words came in a harsh whisper, 'He was no man.'

He knew that she was near the end of her tether. If he continued to turn the screw she would break down and he would be able to extract from her any admission he chose, but he had no stomach for the task. The room, the house, had a stultifying effect on him. Somehow he felt that whatever he did or did not do events would proceed to the same conclusion. It was as though a scenario written twenty years before still dictated their course, including his part in them.

Did she sense his reluctance, his uncertainty? At any rate her attitude hardened again. 'There is no point in you coming here pestering me with your questions. Whatever you say about what happened twenty years ago, you've got no proof and you're no more entitled to make accusations than anybody else. Perhaps I should get my solicitor to do something.'

Wycliffe looked at her blankly and said nothing. His attitude worried her and she wondered if she had gone too far. She tried to draw back.

'You can understand how I feel. I mean, we've got nothing out of it, nothing!' Tears ran down her thin, pale cheeks.

Wycliffe had already moved to the door and he preceded her down the stairs which creaked under his weight.

'What are you going to do?'

He looked at her vaguely. 'Probably nothing at the moment.' He glimpsed her husband's furtive figure at the end of the hall, poised, ready to scuttle back into safety. The cat was back in his place and the trippers and tourists had come out of hiding. Wycliffe walked down the steps and joined the parade.

Bare-footed girls in bikinis and young men in briefs queued with the children for ice-cream. Skinny boys dived off the steps into the harbour, screaming in competition with the gulls. He noticed that the *Marie-Jo* was back, the shabby little half-decked launch on which he had seen a boy and a girl eating a meal of boiled fish. He had sentimentalized over them.

No doubt he attracted some attention as he strolled along the wharf. By now, most of the villagers would know who he was and they would not all have kept it to themselves. In any case he was not dressed—or undressed—for the part of a holiday-maker of the seventies. His light-weight grey suit, pearl-grey shirt and tie might have gone well with a Panama hat to fit into the holiday scene of the twenties.

He made for the telephone box where a youth, propped against the coin box, carried on a conversation which lasted fifteen minutes. When he got inside Wycliffe looked up a number and dialled.

'Father Nesbitt?'

'Speaking. Who is that?' A cautious, priestly voice.

Wycliffe introduced himself and apologized for the intrusion. 'I want to get in touch with a Miss Ella Jordan who once lived here. It occurred to me that you might be able to help me.'

'What about Miss Jordan?'

'I think that she may be able to give me some information.'

'Miss Jordan is an old lady.'

'She is not dead?' Foolishly.

The priest was suave. 'I think not, she was at Mass on Sunday.'

'Then perhaps you will let me have her address.'

A pause. 'I hope that you do not intend to harass her, Chief Superintendent?'

'That is not my intention.' Stiffly.

'You wish to speak to her yourself?'

'If that can be arranged.'

Another pause, longer this time. 'I have a mid-week Mass at

155

seven thirty; if you would care to come along to the presbytery at about eight I will take you to her.' He seemed to think that more was required and added, 'I would like to be there when you talk to Miss Jordan, she is very easily upset.'

'I have no objection.'

'Good! At eight, then.'

Wycliffe was puzzled by the priest's obvious concern.

Back at the hotel the proprietress was at the reception desk, making out bills.

'Any messages for me?'

'Not messages, Chief Superintendent, but there are two young persons waiting to see you. They arrived an hour ago and insisted on waiting. I put them in the TV lounge as few of our guests wish to watch the television at this time of day.'

He found them sitting side by side on one of the settees, holding hands. They were dressed alike in faded blue jeans and checked shirts; the pair from the *Marie-Jo*.

The boy spoke. 'We've got a boat—'

'I know, the *Marie-Jo*, I've seen her in the basin.'

'We came of our own accord.' The boy was on the defensive.

'I'm sure you did. You're Joe—Joe what?'

'Masters, Joe Masters, this is Marie Clark.'

'Not married, then?'

'We intend to be.'

'Good. Now, what do you have to tell me?'

'You tell him, Marie.'

She had not opened her lips so far. Wycliffe was reminded of a popular framed print which had hung in his mother's sitting-room called Sea Dreams. A girl with sun-bleached hair, standing against a background of a fishing village and a windy, blue sky.

'It was Sunday, we were in the basin and we'd settled for the night but I couldn't sleep, it was too hot in the cabin. I went out into the well to get some air and I sat there watching the water. I saw him sculling out from the quay.'

'Who did you see?'

'I couldn't make out his face or anything about him except that he looked tall. It was dark.'

'What time was this?'

She frowned and smoothed the golden hairs on her bare arm. 'I can't say exactly. It was not much short of high tide, probably about three or a bit earlier.'

'Where did he go?'

'He sculled out astern of us and boarded one of the launches. I couldn't see which because it was too dark and in the morning I didn't think any more about it, but whichever it was she was moored about twenty yards from us.'

'Did you form any impression of what he was doing?'

'Not really. I didn't pay a lot of attention. I assumed that he was going out and I think, unconsciously, I was waiting to hear him start up the motor but he didn't.'

'Did you hear anything?'

She shook her head. 'Nothing much. I suppose I must have heard something but it didn't register.'

'He didn't see you?'

'I don't think he can have done. I didn't see him much, just a glimpse now and then, you know how it is on the water, it's never quite dark but it was nearly.'

'How long did he stay aboard?'

Again the frown. 'It's difficult to say but not longer than fifteen minutes, probably not as long.'

'Then he sculled back to the quay?'

'Yes.'

'You say he was tall. Was he thin or fat?'

'Not fat.' She was obviously doing her best. 'I think at night, on the water, things look taller and thinner than they really are, I don't know why. Well, this man looked that way but I couldn't be sure that he really was.'

Wycliffe tried but he could get nothing more. The girl had told him all she had seen.

'What made you come to see me now? Why didn't you come forward earlier?'

The boy took over. 'Well, we'd heard about the murder, of course, but we don't read the newspapers or listen to the news on the radio so we didn't know any details. It was only this morning when Marie bought some vegetables wrapped in an old newspaper that we read about what had actually happened and then Marie remembered what she had seen.'

'So we thought we'd better come and tell somebody,' the girl said. 'We asked on the quay and one of the men told us that you were in charge.'

'I'm glad you came,' Wycliffe said. He thanked them and personally conducted them through the foyer under the eyes of the proprietress. He stood, watching them walk off down the drive, still hand in hand.

Helen and Ruth arrived back at six o'clock and he had to admire a dress for Ruth and a pair of shoes for Helen. He acquired two pairs of socks and a new toothbrush. The consumer society.

'You're looking better, dear.'

'I feel better.'

So there was scarcely a protest when he broke the news that he would skip the evening meal.

At a quarter to eight he drove the five or six miles to the church and arrived there as people were coming out from the service. He could see the priest standing in the little pseudo-Gothic porch, shaking hands with his congregation as they filed out. The organ was still playing and he was reminded of summer Sunday evenings in his boyhood when, in a grey suit with a school badge on the pocket and a school cap on his head he walked to chapel between his father and mother. 'Raise your cap to Mrs Soper, Charles!' Then the seemingly interminable service with the sun streaming in through the big west window making the faces of the girls in the choir glow so that they looked prettier. As he remembered them they all wore powder-blue summer coats and little toque hats of the same colour.

When the last of the congregation had gone he left the car and walked over to the priest who waited for him. He was a tall, thin man in the late fifties or early sixties with close-cropped grey hair, strong features and rather cold grey eyes. A severe man who had long since made his final assessments of the world, the flesh and the devil.

He was led through the church where the sacristan was snuffing candles on the altar and the organist was locking up. A little door to the left of the choir led through a short passage into a small, tiled hall from which several doors opened.

'If you will wait in here, Chief Superintendent.'

He was shown into the priest's study. A desk with a telephone, a *prie-dieu* with a crucifix above it, bookshelves, a couple of not-too-comfortable chairs and a threadbare carpet. Here the three odours of piety were blended—pitchpine, incense and hassocks. He was not kept waiting long. Father Nesbitt came back having changed out of his vestments into a long clerical coat.

'It is not far, we can easily walk.'

Ella Jordan lived in a little terraced house on a hill overlooking the town. The houses were built only on one side and on the other, after a low, stone wall, the ground dropped steeply. As they walked the priest seemed to be preparing the ground.

'I have half expected to hear from you. You must not be hard on her. If you had been doing my job for forty years you would realize that you have to come to terms with human frailty.' This to a detective superintendent.

Wycliffe had his work cut out keeping up with the priest's long, rapid strides which were scarcely moderated as they began to feel the slope of the hill.

'Here we are, number twenty-seven.'

A little glass porch filled with geraniums in all shades from pink to dark red. Nesbitt pushed open the inner door and called, 'Miss Jordan! It is I, Father Nesbitt. Don't disturb yourself, I am coming through. I've brought you a visitor.'

The little room at the back was so dark that at first Wycliffe could see nothing, but as his eyes accommodated he saw a little old lady sitting in a wicker chair with a cat on her lap. She spoke in a strong though cracked voice.

'You must excuse me, Father, I would have got up but I don't want to disturb Timmy, he's having such a nice sleep.' She looked at Wycliffe. 'Who's this, then?'

Nesbitt placed a wooden kitchen chair for Wycliffe and another for himself. 'This is Mr Wycliffe, he's a policeman and he's anxious to talk to you.'

Her voice became wary. 'What about?'

Wycliffe cleared his throat, not at all sure of his ground. 'About something which happened more than twenty years ago, Miss Jordan, when you were living with your half-sister.'

She said nothing but a tiny mottled hand began to smooth the cat's black fur.

'You remember Alice Weekes being murdered?'

'Of course I remember, I'm not gone soft in the head yet.'

'I have read a transcript of the statements made to the police at the time and of the evidence given at the trial, you seem to have been left out.'

'They didn't ask me anything. If they had done—'

'If they had done—what?'

'I think I would have told them.' Her voice seemed to catch on the words and she raised a hand to her lips.

She shifted her position in the chair and the wicker strands creaked. The cat woke, stretched himself precariously and slid off on to the floor.

'Father knows all about it and I promised, didn't I, Father?'

'You promised.' The priest's voice was calming and reassuring.

'I wrote the letter and sent it.'

'A letter?'

'Father Nesbitt wrote another letter to go with it.'

'To whom was the letter sent?'

'Why, to Morley, of course. You must have seen it, else why did you come?'

Wycliffe shook his head. 'I have seen no letter.'

Light was almost totally excluded from the little room by the steeply rising ground behind the house but the front rooms must have been flooded with the evening sun.

The priest was caught off balance. 'Naturally I thought . . . In the circumstances . . .'.

The old lady was in no doubt. 'I said I would speak out if ever I was asked and I will.' She paused, apparently searching for words which would not come then she said, 'You tell him, Father.'

The priest placed the tips of his white fingers together and studied them.

'Four—almost five years ago, Miss Jordan was very ill—'

'I had a blockage.'

'In privileged circumstances she told me of events which had occurred many years before of which she claimed to have guilty knowledge.'

The priest was picking his words very carefully. 'If her interpretation of the events was correct she had allowed a young man to go to prison for a crime he did not commit.' The white hands made a slight gesture. 'With her permission I made certain enquiries and I learned that the man, now no longer young, had been released; he had completed his sentence.' He became even more cautious and deliberate. 'Miss Jordan decided to acquaint him with what she knew and she put her account of the events into writing. Then, in case Miss Jordan failed to recover, I appended a brief statement saying that the account had been written of her own free will and in my presence.'

'And all this was sent to Morley Tremain?'

'Yes.'

'You advised her to do this?'

'As one of two or three possibilities.'

'You realize that—?' Wycliffe started to speak but broke off. What was the use?

In any case the priest knew what he had been on the point of saying.

'I prayed for guidance.'

'Did you hear from Tremain?'

'We heard nothing.'

'You have a copy of what was written?'

161

'No.'

'And that was nearly five years ago?'

'August '69!' Unexpectedly from Ella Jordan. 'I went into hospital on the 24th July and I came home on the 4th September.'

'Morley Tremain must have received this remarkable communication while he was living quietly with his mother in Southampton.'

In the silence there was a faint mewing from an adjoining room.

'That's Timmy, he wants to go out.' Ella Jordan got up and bustled out of the room. 'I won't be a minute.'

'A remarkable woman,' Wycliffe said.

She came back and switched on the electric light at the door. 'No need to be here in the gloaming.'

The yellow light did little to brighten the little room in which the prevailing colour was brown.

Ella went back to her chair; she was cocooned in woollen garments in all shades. Dusty black stockings were wrinkled about her ankles and she wore carpet slippers which were too big for her.

'I shall have to ask you some questions.'

'When I heard that Harry had been killed I knew it would all come out. It was Cedric; that boy was vicious—vicious and wicked and his mother ruined him. From a little boy . . . I remember when he couldn't have been more than five he was out in the backyard throwing stones at a little puppy his mother had bought for him. And what did she do . . . ? Now he's gone and killed his own father.'

'Miss Jordan, I want to ask you a question and you should be very careful how you answer. Are you saying that Cedric and not Morley Tremain murdered Alice Weekes?'

'Of course that's what I'm saying, it's true.'

'Do you have proof?'

She looked at him with surprise in her eyes which were bright though sunken. 'I was there, wasn't I . . . ?'

'Tell me what happened.'

She wiped her nose with a grubby rag. 'It was a Sunday and Sunday was my day off. I used to catch the bus and come over here to go to Mass. That was before Father Nesbitt's time; it was Father . . . Father . . .'

'Father Boyle,' the priest supplied.

'That's right, Father Boyle. Well, as I was saying, I went to Mass, then I would go home with Mary Finn and have a bite of dinner at her place before I got the three o'clock bus back. I did that for years. Mary's dead now, poor soul . . .' Her eyes glazed over as her thoughts were clouded by memories.

Wycliffe had to prompt her.

'When I got back I could see something was wrong. There'd been a row. There was an atmosphere, you could feel it. Well, I went up to take my things off and when I come down again, just to cheer things up like, I said, "What about a cup of tea?"

'I'll never forget it. Harry was standing by the window, smoking his pipe, Eunice had the paper spread out on the kitchen table, reading, Clara was fiddling about with something on the dresser and, o' course, the old man was sitting in his usual chair by the fire. Before anybody had a chance to answer me, master Cedric comes bursting in . . .'

The recollection clearly excited her, her upper lip, furrowed by wrinkles and sprouting long, white hairs like vibrissae, was trembling.

'He was white as a sheet, panting and shouting like a mad thing. "I've killed her! I've killed her!" He kept shouting it and they couldn't stop him until his mother went over and slapped him hard, across his face. Then he started to cry.

'Clara never batted an eyelid. She put her arm round him and talked to him like he was a baby, and after a minute or two, although he was still sobbing, she got him to go upstairs with her. We was left there in the kitchen, Harry, Eunice and me. And of course, the old man was there but you couldn't count him because he was as good as dead already.' The scene had impressed itself on her memory so indelibly that she could describe it as though it were still before her eyes.

'The funny thing was, none of us moved for a long time. Harry was standing with his back to the window, holding his pipe, I was by the dresser with a dish in my hand and Eunice was sat at the table with a Sunday newspaper spread out in front of her. There used to be an old clock on the mantelpiece over the stove with all sorts of knobs and carvings and I can hear it ticking now. Then Eunice said, "I better go up," but her father said, "You stay where you are, my girl, and leave it to your mother!"

'After that we pretended to go on normal but, of course, we was only waiting and it was more than an hour before Clara come down as cool as a cucumber. She looked round at the three of us then she said, "Ceddie is poorly and I've put him to bed."

'Eunice said, "But what about—? What about what he said?" And his mother snapped back, "I never heard him say a thing, he was crying. I don't know what's the matter with him but he's very poorly."

'Nobody said another word but when it was time for me to go and catch my bus to go to church she said, "I think it would be better if you didn't go tonight, Ella; what with Ceddie being unwell I might be glad of you being here." '

The old lady pursed her almost bloodless lips and looked from Wycliffe to the priest and back again. There could be no question but that she was enjoying herself.

'Next day, which was a Monday, Harry was away to sea early, Cedric was still in bed and Clara, Eunice and me had given the boarders their breakfasts and we was having our breakfast before Clara and me went up to bring the old man down. When we'd finished and I was going to start clearing away, Clara said, "Wait a minute!" She kept us sitting there, watching her, for a long time then she said, "Yesterday Cedric had a stomach upset after dinner, it must have been something he ate, and he was in bed for the rest of the day, he never went out after dinner." You should have seen her eyes! "Yesterday he didn't go outside that door after one o'clock."

'Neither Eunice nor me dared speak. When Eunice went out to do the shopping she heard that Alice Weekes' body had been found in the old engine-house, and she told me but she never said a word to her mother and it was never mentioned in my hearing. All that happened was that three or four times during the next couple of days Clara would say when we was together, "On Sunday Cedric was in bed with a bilious attack . . . All afternoon and evening . . . He never went outside that door . . ." '

She sighed and leaned back, her tiny, deformed hands resting on the wicker arms of her chair. 'And all through the trial not a word was spoken in that house about it, not a word.' She nodded her head several times in silence. 'Even when the police come to the house there was nothing said. I could see it was preying on Harry, he went to look ten year older in a few weeks . . .'

'Why did you not tell the police at the time?'

She screwed up her lips. 'I wasn't asked, was I?'

'You know that is no answer.'

She smoothed the clothes over her knees. 'I was dependent. I had nothing more than they gave me. I know it was wicked and I've never ceased to ask the Blessed Virgin to intercede for me.'

'And this money you came into?'

'I never came into no money. Who would leave me money? They couldn't bear having me round the place after what I knew and so Harry bought me this little house and give me the deeds and every month he would come here and leave it on the sideboard in an envelope.'

'Leave what on the sideboard?'

'Two five-pound notes.'

'How long did this go on?'

'He was here the beginning of June and he'd have been here the first of July if he'd lived. Of course, ten pounds isn't what it was but I got my pension and with no rent I'm comfortable enough.'

She looked round her little room with satisfaction. 'Of course, I don't know what'll happen now with Harry gone but I could still manage. When you're old you don't want much.'

Wycliffe looked at the priest who was sitting bolt upright, his palms matched and his finger-tips to his lips.

The priest said, 'I suppose you'll want a statement?'

'I don't know.'

The priest looked surprised but said nothing.

Wycliffe left them together and walked back to the car alone. The sun had set but the sky in the west was barred with orange and gold clouds. When he reached the village it was already dusk.

Chapter Eleven

WALTER TYSON WAS making his nightly inspection of
the camping site. It was the time of day he liked best. The sun
had set and darkness seemed to sift gently out of the sky like a
fine dust, softening outlines and dimming the brash colours of
the tents so that they were reduced to vague geometrical shapes.
There were lights in some of the caravans and shadows on the
curtains; children being put to bed in high bunks. An hour before
he had switched on the lighting but this was confined to the main
avenue and the wash-ups. As he walked round nobody would
stare at him or look quickly away when they caught his eye. He
felt protected by the darkness. A few family groups were still
sitting outside, their faces no more than pale blurs, and they
talked little.

'Good night, Mr Tyson.' A man exercising his dog. They got
to know him after two or three days on the site. He liked that.

It was a well-conducted site and he was proud of it.

He stopped to replace a plastic lid on a refuse bin; a little
further on the tap on a standpipe had been left dribbling and he
turned it off. A man sat on the steps of his caravan smoking a
cigarette. Behind him his wife, in a blue dressing-gown, was
putting a saucepan on to the gas hot-plate.

'Good night.'

He arrived at the wash-ups and strolled between the rows of
white sinks. He made a mental note of a pane of broken glass
in one of the windows. He looked into the men's toilets and, after
a questioning call, into the women's. All in order.

From the wash-ups to the permanent vans. Lights in all but
one—number eight. The occupants of number eight had left
without giving him notice after they had been questioned by the

police superintendent. He would have given a lot to have known what had been said.

In number six they were watching television, he could see the pale flicker from the set reflected on the ceiling. Then he came to the tents. From some of them there was a soft glow through the canvas. In one a baby was whimpering and in another a radio was playing softly. Except for number eight everything was as it should have been.

He opened the door of his own van and switched on the light. The stainless steel sink and the electric kettle gleamed. He put a saucepan of milk on the hot-plate to make himself some cocoa. So practised was he that the milk he had put into the saucepan exactly filled his mug. He took his drink through into the living-room where plastic, imitation wood veneers showed not a single smear. He sat in an easy chair upholstered in orange velvet, picked up his current library book, opened it at the marker and started to read, sipping his drink from time to time. The clock on the wall showed eleven. At half-past eleven he got up and went to the shelf-unit which occupied almost the whole of one side of the room. He switched on the radio, set it to Radio 3 and waited for the news which was due at 11.35. He was working, as always, to a strict timetable which only varied to suit the vagaries of the radio schedules.

Northern Ireland, a prison break-out, a grim warning from the Shadow Chancellor about the economic plight of the country, a footballer's sex life and the weather. He switched off with a sigh of relief.

It seemed to him now that the days of his second lease of life were numbered, he was living on borrowed time. Each evening when he came in from his routine patrol and switched on the news he would chalk up, mentally, one more day. It gave him a sense of achievement but it could not go on for much longer. This police superintendent was biding his time. Several times he had been conscious of those soft, expressionless eyes, watching him. On one occasion he had been on the point of throwing in the towel, getting it over with. He had even formulated the words that he would use, 'This is how it was . . .' Now, whenever he re-called that moment, he came out in a cold sweat, for it would not have been the end and he could not face re-entering that grey limbo of existence where he had spent so much of his life.

Now he had reached a decision and he had a plan, an insurance. But the plan depended on him having a little warning. He must not be caught unawares.

He tidied the living-room as he always did before going to bed. While he was doing so a car with a defective silencer roared past his van accompanied by shrieks and laughter. He knew the party, two young men and two girls who had arrived the previous evening in a blue sports car with a tent they did not know how to put up. They were unruly, not the kind he wanted on the site. He would speak to them in the morning.

He took his empty cocoa mug through to the kitchen, washed it and the saucepan and put them both away.

Wycliffe spent a restless night. Between dreaming and waking he created in his imagination a disturbing reconstruction of the events Ella Jordan had described. When he had heard the story, told with the shameless, amoral detachment of an old woman, it had seemed to him sinister and depressing; now, recollected between tumbled and sweaty sheets, it took on the quality of nightmare. Clara Tremain, obsessively, implacably protective, her eyes hard and cold, pursued him into his dreams. It was already getting light when he fell into a deep sleep and when he woke it took him some time to realize where he was.

'Is it going to be fine?'

They were having breakfast. Helen and Ruth had arranged to go with the Wordens to visit a nearby estate, owned by the National Trust.

'Why don't you come? You can hardly say that the motion upsets you.' She was teasing him, of course, but he was so deeply absorbed in what had become 'his case' that he answered her testily,

'No, I can't possibly.'

He was on edge because he was waiting.

After breakfast he went out into the foyer and stood, mooning about, smoking his pipe. Helen and Ruth went off to join the Wordens; the other guests came down in couples or in groups to start another day of their holidays. The proprietress, in and out of Reception, watched him, or so he thought, with a resentful eye.

'I'm expecting a telephone call. I shall be in my room.'

He had a vague sense of urgency which he could not explain. A confused memory of the thoughts and dreams which had disturbed his rest made him uneasy. He fancied that he had seen a clear need for a certain course of action but he could not now remember what it was. In a 'real' case he would have been absorbed in routine work and he would have had no time to get temperamental.

In his room he sat in the wicker chair by the window and tried to sort out his ideas but he found himself watching the pleasure boats crossing the bay, a veritable armada, on their way to Seal Island and Gull Rock. The sea was dark blue and choppy, the sky overhead a lighter blue with spindrifts of white cloud, a windy sky.

A quarter of an hour after he had left it he was back in the foyer.

'I'm going out. If anyone calls please tell them that I will ring back.'

'Certainly, Chief Superintendent.'

He left the hotel and walked, the long way round, to the square. Housewives were doing their shopping and vans were unloading supplies of fruit, vegetables and groceries. A gusty wind blew litter on to the pavements and made the women button their woolly cardigans. Getting weather-wise, Wycliffe would have been prepared to bet that there was rain in the wind. He turned right along the main street and looked with special interest at the shop on the corner where Morley Tremain had been born forty-three years ago. He would have liked to have seen the rooms where the Tremains had lived but he had no possible excuse. He walked as far as the stone-shop and stopped to look in the window. As far as he could see over the curtain the shop appeared to be empty. He went inside and a bell sounded somewhere as he opened the door. He stood looking at the glass cases in which stones, polished and unpolished, mounted and unmounted, were displayed. From a back room came the continuous grating sound of a tumbling machine at work.

It was some time before the woman he had supposed to be Cedric's wife came through into the shop. She was wearing a white, nylon overall which emphasized her dark colouring; her jet black hair and warm skin looked like an advertisement for sun-tan lotion. It was difficult to see her as a woman of thirty-nine.

No introductions were needed, although they had not met she knew who he was. Her manner was relaxed.

'I've been expecting you or one of your men, Chief Superintendent.'

The words were ordinary but the manner in which she spoke them was warm and subtly flattering as though she had not only expected but looked forward to the encounter. Evidently a woman who had cultivated the art of charming men. With such women Wycliffe became, quite unintentionally, gruff, almost rude. He was always slightly embarrassed by social skills which he could neither relish nor emulate.

'Could I have a word privately?'

She looked round the empty shop then smiled. 'You'd better come through.' She walked over to the shop door and dropped the catch. 'I shan't miss the custom we get at this time of day.'

Wycliffe followed her through a stockroom and workshop up carpeted stairs to the flat above. He was taken into a little sitting-room which had a restricted view of the harbour between houses on the front. The room was neat, subdued and plain, fawn and dark brown. Through an open door he could see into the bed-room and a man's slippers by the foot of the bed. She saw the direction of his glance, closed the door and pointed to a chair.

'I have a man-friend, I make no secret of it.'

'Is he the reason you left your husband?'

'No, when I met him I was already living here. He's a sales rep and he's married. As far as I know he intends to stay that way.'

She went to a little marquetry table and took a cigarette from a box. 'Want one?'

Wycliffe refused.

'I put up with Cedric until my daughter, Laura, was old enough to fend for herself and until I had enough money to set up on my own.'

'Why did you marry him in the first place?'

She was not offended by his directness. 'The short answer is that I was pregnant.' She smoked elegantly; in fact, everything she did was done with a controlled grace. Remembering Laura, Wycliffe thought that the girl must have studied to be as different from her mother as possible but there was no disguising the affinity of face, figure and voice. Wycliffe was also conscious of the same air of amused tolerance which had piqued him in the daughter.

'Of course, that wasn't the whole story. Cedric had a way with women and he could have had his pick.' She smiled a little dourly. 'I suppose he did. Anyway, at the time I thought that I was lucky. We were married in July 1953, when I was eighteen.'

'You never had a second child?'

'No.'

'You have money of your own?'

'A legacy from an aunt. That was what finally made it possible for me to walk out on Cedric. Without that I should have had to think twice.'

She sat, relaxed, attentive, her long legs lightly crossed.

'You are not asking me about my father-in-law.'

'Would you be able to tell me anything if I did?'

She smiled. 'Nothing you don't already know, but I understood that it was the way of the police to make everybody say the same thing at least three times.'

'Were you surprised to hear that your daughter had inherited his money?'

'Very, but I'm glad for her. I hope that she will be sensible.'
It was impossible not to be impressed by her cool objectivity.
Wycliffe looked round the sitting-room, not a speck of dust anywhere, not a cushion out of place. The pictures on the walls —watercolours of landscapes—were of uniform size, all framed alike in Hogarth moulding with white mounts. What did he want from her? He sat in his chair, vaguely benign while she watched him, alert, incisive and curious.

'I suppose you were born in the village?'

'My father was one of the Bray brothers, the firm which bought all the fish landed at the port. They were in difficulties at the time of my marriage and they hoped that Harry Tremain would back them.'

'Did he?'

'Not on your life! Although he had been born and bred a fisherman, he wasn't putting his money in anything so unpredictable.'

'What happened?'

'They went broke in the early sixties.'

'You must have known Morley Tremain?'

'Morley?' She looked surprised. 'Of course I knew him. He was a bit older than me but we travelled on the same bus to school every day.'

'What sort of a boy was he?'

She frowned. 'Quiet. A bit of a mummy's boy. He didn't mix much and I suspect that he was bullied.'

'The sort of chap you would expect to rape and murder?'

She looked at him, half smiling. 'What is this? You are the detective but you ask me the sort of boy who is likely to rape and murder?'

He nodded. 'I'm still asking.'

She considered, seriously. 'Well, no. But aren't the quiet introverts the very ones who . . .?'

'Perhaps. So you were never in any doubt of his guilt?'

'No, it never entered my head.'

'Why did he kill her?'

173

She was growing increasingly puzzled. 'Why? Jealousy, I suppose. She was his girl and he found her with another man.'

'With Cedric.'

'All right, with Cedric. But I don't see what you are getting at.'

He was silent for a while, staring out of the window at the backs of the houses on the waterfront. From where he sat he could see the top-floor windows of The Quay House rising above the other roofs.

'You were already married when Morley Tremain came to trial and it became public knowledge that Cedric had been with the dead girl.'

She shrugged. 'What of it? It was no news to me nor to anyone else in the village that Cedric would go with any girl.' She stubbed out her cigarette. 'Girls are strange animals, Mr Wycliffe. Look at Laura. With all her chances she goes with a married man old enough to be her father.'

She sat looking at him with an expression which was puzzled but unconcerned. She did not understand his interest in the events of twenty years ago but she was not troubled by his questions.

'I suppose it's too early to offer you a drink?'

He agreed absentmindedly. 'In the evidence at the trial it was said that Cedric was taken ill after lunch on the day of the murder and that he went to bed and stayed there.'

A very faint smile. 'He was drunk.'

'Drunk?'

'I was out with him the evening before. He knew that I was going to have a baby and he had promised to marry me but he wouldn't tell his father. Well, I issued an ultimatum—if he didn't, I would. So he told his father that Sunday morning.'

There was a ghost of a twinkle in her eye.

'Harry Tremain never lost his temper but he had a way of making his point which was far more effective. He could always be relied upon to reduce Cedric to drivelling incoherence in minutes. I gather that he excelled himself that Sunday morning and, of course, Cedric went out and got drunk. That was, and remained, his sovereign remedy for all ills. When the pubs closed I suppose he went home and went to bed.'

'You are sure of all this?'

She was puzzled by his doubt. Her dark, intelligent eyes searched his face. 'Of course I'm sure. My brother was in the bar of the Robartes that lunch-time and he came home and told me that Cedric was there, drowning his sorrows, already drunk enough to be ugly.'

She paused, then added, 'What are you getting at?'

Wycliffe made a vague gesture. 'Just one more question. After the murder, did you notice any change in Cedric?'

She hesitated. 'Well, it was only three weeks afterwards that we got married. I expected him to change.'

'But was the change greater than you expected?'

She could not understand his grave persistence.

'Well, yes. To be honest, he was far more upset by the murder than I would have expected. I don't think he had much feeling for the girl but it was Morley... I must say I was surprised by the effect it had on him.' She smoothed the skirt of her overall. 'In some ways he was never quite the same man again; it changed him.'

'In sexual matters?'

A brief pause. 'Yes. I can't imagine why you want to know all this but in that way too.'

'He was less... effective?'

'Yes. As far as that was concerned I came to the conclusion that now the fruit was no longer forbidden it had lost its attraction.'

'Did he continue to seek novelty elsewhere?'

'I don't think he did, not at any rate for several years.'

Wycliffe stood up. She looked up at him and, for the first time, her eyes were troubled. 'I hope that what I have told you will do him no harm?'

Wycliffe regarded her for some time before he answered. 'I think I can promise you that.' Then he added, 'Thank you for your help.'

She smiled doubtfully. 'Frankly, I can't see what you're getting at.'

'Neither can I.'

He reached the end of the street where shops gave way to cottages and the road started to rise steeply and to turn inland. A final alley led off on the left and he went along it to come out by the slate-fronted house which was Eunice's despised inheritance. The sky was clouding over and Wycliffe thought that he felt spots of rain. He went up the granite steps and once more banged with his knuckles on the front door. Once more Eunice came out of the kitchen at the end of the stone passage. This time her hands were covered in flour. She looked even thinner, the bones of her skull and face seemed scarcely covered by the flesh.

'What is it now?'

'I've been talking to Ella Jordan.'

She turned away and he followed her down the passage to the kitchen where she had a yeast-cake mixture in a bowl on the table.

'I thought she was dead.'

'Your father bought a house for her and he's been giving her ten pounds a month for the past twenty years. Why should he do that?'

She went on, kneading the dough, and did not answer.

'In what circumstances did she leave here?'

'Circumstances? She was weak in the head and you never knew what she was going to say or do next. It got so that mother couldn't stand her around the house any longer and I suppose father thought they owed her something. He told me that she'd come into a bit of money.'

Although her hands moved through the dough with a purely mechanical movement she never once lifted her eyes from the bowl. The solid fuel stove was at baking heat and Wycliffe could feel the perspiration breaking out all over his body.

Wycliffe had seated himself on a cane-bottomed chair and the cat came, rubbing itself round his legs and purring like a well-oiled engine.

'If you had your time to go over again would you give the same evidence at your cousin's trial?'

For an instant he thought that she was going to break down, but she kept control.

'Of course, it was the truth.' But she could not resist adding, 'If anybody is telling you different they're filthy liars!'

He would have found it very difficult to explain why he had made these morning visits. The truth was that he had almost decided on a course of action and he needed to bolster his confidence. He would have liked to talk to Cedric also but that was not practicable, at least not in circumstances which would make it worthwhile.

Once more he was back on the quay; the morning lingered indecisively between rain and shine and there were fewer people about than usual. He went over to the telephone box and dialled the number of his hotel.

'Wycliffe here. Has there been a call for me? ... No, thank you, I will look in after lunch ...'

He walked across to the quay rail and stood, with his arms on the rail, staring down into the water. A few days ago he had never heard of these people, then they became characters in a bizarre tragedy reported by the newspapers. Now, he was beginning to know them. Even Cedric whom he had never seen and Cedric's father who was dead.

Eunice in her slate house with her adored son and her compliant husband. At least she could maintain a front of respectability.

Laura, now a rich young woman, having an affair with her boss who was old enough to be her father.

Laura's mother, settling gracefully for her stone-shop and her itinerant lover.

Ella Jordan, living out her last years in modest comfort within easy reach of the consoling ministrations of the Church.

Cedric, a sick man, in prison, awaiting trial for the murder of his father.

Harry Tremain himself. In the long tradition of hard-headed

puritans who have mastered the story of the talents if little else in the Gospels. But Harry is dead.

And Walter Tyson . . .

Wycliffe could see them all with disturbing clarity but he found it difficult to *think* about them.

It was still only half-past eleven and he decided to go for a walk. He was on the cliffs by the old engine-house when they started to blast at the quarry. The first shot was timed for mid-day and he, like the villagers, had come to regard it as one of the landmarks of his day. It was a signal now for him to turn back to the village if he was going to lunch with the doctor. But before turning back he entered the ruin to see the enclosed square of grass where Alice Weekes had met her death. It was inaccessible, overgrown with brambles. Alice's death had almost certainly put a stop to couples coming there and, as Eunice had said, the old mine road—the top path—was overgrown also.

For once he was first into the dining-room. When the doctor arrived he was studying the menu.

'Sauté chicken with cauliflower and croquettes.'

'Suits me, what shall we drink?'

'No wine for me today; if it's all the same to you, I would prefer a lager.' He wanted something light, he felt mentally and physically oppressed.

'Soup?'

'Not for me.'

The doctor raised his eyebrows. 'Liverish?'

'Could be.'

'Take some exercise.'

When they had almost finished the main course, Wycliffe said, 'I suppose you have had the job of telling someone that he or she was going to die?'

'It's happened to every GP more than once.'

'How do they take it?'

The doctor was watching him quizzically. 'Quietly; I've never known anybody break down in those circumstances.'

'If you could have offered them fourteen or fifteen years in gaol, instead, do you think they would have taken the option?'

'Are you one of the "bring back the rope" brigade?'

'I asked you a question.'

'I don't know the answer. I think in most cases it would probably be yes.'

'Because they don't know what it's like in gaol.'

'While there's life, there's hope. Hackneyed but true.' The doctor was consulting the menu again. 'I'm tempted by the cherry tart with cream.'

'No sweet for me.'

The doctor was looking at him with a hint of amusement which added to his annoyance. He was annoyed with himself because his own behaviour struck him as so absurd. Whenever he had to make a decision which deeply involved his conscience or when he was facing a crisis he denied himself something. No soup, no wine, no cherry tart... How stupid can you get? As a child when he was going to the dentist or to communion at chapel or to school on examination days he would carefully avoid stepping on the lines between the paving stones... But a grown man!

He ordered coffee and drank it down while it was still too hot.

'Is Cedric your patient?'

'Yes.'

'Then I suppose you will tell me nothing about his health?'

A knowing look from the doctor. 'I don't mind telling you that he's got a dicky heart and that he might go at any time.'

'Thanks. Well, I must be off.'

'In a hurry?'

When he came out on to the quay it was raining and the wind was slanting the rain so that it beat against the fronts of the houses and the shops. It was just before two when he arrived back at his hotel. The rheumy-eyed porter was behind the desk.

'There's a message for you, sir. Madam says you're to ring the Southampton number any time from a quarter past two on.'

He went up to his room and at a quarter past two precisely he put through his call.

Chief Inspector Chubb was apologetic. 'Sorry it's taken so long but the crash was outside our manor... On the A3 at War Down, three or four miles south of Petersfield... January '71. The roads were bad. A lorry hit a petrol tanker amidships and there was petrol seeping on to the road. Then along comes this clapped-out old van and skids into that lot... Three men travelling in the van, the driver and two others. The driver was crushed by the steering column and the other two went through the windshield. One of them, your man, Tremain, was killed outright, the driver died in hospital but a third chap recovered eventually, though, from what I gather, he was in a hell of a state. The petrol on the road caught alight and it was bloody lucky the tanker didn't... Wait a minute, I've got it here... Tyson, Walter Tyson... It seems the two had thumbed a lift just north of Petersfield... It turned out that they shared a room in some bugpit in Pompey... Out of work, both of 'em... No, as far as I know, no relatives were ever traced. Tremain had a wallet on him with his dole card and three quid... Don't mention it, I hope it's some use. We must get together for a jar some time.'

Wycliffe thanked him and replaced the receiver.

It seemed to him that the pattern was now complete and the day had provided him with two more vivid mind-images, both of them aspects of violence.

Cedric Tremain, fuddled and resentful, unwilling to face his father, putting off the moment. Alice, fresh from her encounter with Morley. She tries to shake Cedric off but he is drunkenly persistent. Then his aggression focuses in a sudden randy impulse but she resists.

What's got into the bloody little scrubber?

He drags her into the old engine-house. Perhaps she screams. Enough of that! That's better. Then the slow awakening...

And the other. A shining wet road in the evening and a lorry jack-knifes into a petrol tanker. A crazy, clapped-out old van skids into both. Glass and petrol and two bodies on the road...

Chapter Twelve

Although it was raining hard and blowing a gale Tyson made his routine inspection of the site. He wore yellow oilskins and Wellington boots. Three or four of the tents were in trouble; not properly sited or not properly put up. Some people would never be told and always knew best until they were in difficulties. He helped one couple to dig a shallow trench round their tent; farther along a big ridge tent had collapsed completely with the occupants inside and he had a struggle to extricate them in the darkness. Before setting out on his rounds he had made sure that all was well in the camp shelter. It was only a bare, concrete room with a few forms and tables but it was dry and there was a vending machine which dispensed hot drinks. It was in this weather that the caravanners came into their own; the little squares of orange light must have seemed the height of comfort and luxury to wet and bedraggled tenters. Not that there was any need to be wet or bedraggled if they took advice.

There was a surface-water drain choked along the main roadway and he had to go back to the store for an iron crook to lift the heavy grating and to prod the blockage. It was while he was at the store that he noticed a big car parked near the entrance with its side-lights burning, but it was not unusual for visitors to the site to leave their cars there. He cleared the drain and made his way back. He put the crook in the store and took off his oilskins and boots, leaving them there to dry, then he hurried across to his own van. The weather was worsening but the van seemed more than ever inviting. He was later than usual so he switched on the radio at once and set about making his cocoa. As he was pouring the milk into the saucepan there was a knock at the door and he went to answer it.

'Mr Wycliffe!'

For the first time in many days he had allowed himself to forget. It was ironical.

Wycliffe came in, his shoulders and trouser legs were damp even from the short walk. 'I saw you setting out on your rounds so I waited.'

The big car must have been parked there for over an hour.

'I thought I might have seen you at the pub in the village.'

Tyson tried to match the superintendent's easy manner. 'Not in this weather, it's too risky to leave the site.'

Wycliffe went through into the living-room. He was carrying a despatch case which he laid on the table and opened. He drew out a buff manilla folder. The folder was labelled with a filing number and the words, 'Morley Tremain. Murder. June 1953' in bold letters and the impress of a rubber stamp added, 'Case closed.'

The man with the disfigured face looked at the file, indeed, it seemed that he could not take his eyes off it, but made no comment and his features were incapable of registering emotion.

Wycliffe looked at him. 'You know what this is?'

'Yes.'

'It contains, amongst other things, your fingerprints.'

'And fourteen years of my life.'

'You are Morley Tremain?'

'Yes.' He looked at the file again, then at Wycliffe. 'I did not kill that girl.'

'I know.'

Tremain accepted the admission as though it were of little consequence now.

Wycliffe looked round then sat in one of the orange, velvet chairs. Tremain, after a glance which seemed to ask permission, sat in the other.

'I want you to answer my questions, Mr Tremain.'

Tremain gave no sign that he had heard.

'You suffered your injuries in a road accident in 1971?'

'Yes.'

'At the time you were with a man who was killed in the accident; that man was Walter Tyson?'

'Yes.'

'Tell me about the events which led up to the accident and the circumstances in which you assumed your companion's identity.' Wycliffe was deliberately dry and precise, he wanted to keep the emotional temperature down.

Tremain made a gesture of helplessness and Wycliffe tried to prompt him.

'Begin after your mother's death when you sold the furniture.'

Tremain was silent for a long time.

'You know that mother took a house and waited for me all the time I was on the island?'

It was Wycliffe's turn to reply with a monosyllable. 'Yes.'

'When I came out I felt that I owed her something and her very first words to me were, "Now we can take up where we left off ..."' He sighed and his deformed nostrils turned the sigh into a ridiculous whistle. 'It was all going to be as if nothing had ever happened. I would get a job, go to work, come home and she would be there to keep house.' He paused, staring at the floral design on the carpet. 'Well, it worked more or less. I made it work. I'd learnt a trade in prison, assembling radios. It turned out that I was very good with my hands and through the Prisoners' Aid I got a job in a factory where they made calculators. Mother was content, at least I think she was, but for me it was like an extension of my sentence.

'You can't know what it's like to spend fourteen years in prison, Mr Wycliffe.'

The words were not an appeal for sympathy but a statement of fact.

'It affects different people in different ways, I suppose, but I just wanted to stop; to stop working, to stop thinking, even to stop living ... Not to have to do *anything*.'

It was one of the strangest experiences of Wycliffe's career. The caravan was buffeted by wind and rain so that, sometimes, it rocked on its supports. But inside all was calm and the man's monotonous voice droned on, carefully, almost painfully enunciating each word.

'When mother died I just packed it in. I cleared out. For a few months I mooned about, often sleeping rough. I reached rock bottom and in a funny sort of way I'd got what I wanted. I can't explain it but for the first time I had no feelings about anything, not even about myself or what would happen to me. I was in Portsmouth at the time and it was then that I met Walter Tyson.' Tremain broke off, 'My mouth is dry, do you think I could have something to drink?'

'It's your home . . .'

Tremain got up and went out into the kitchen. In a moment or two he returned with a pint can of beer and two glasses. He held up the glasses to Wycliffe with an oddly tentative gesture.

'Thanks.'

Tremain opened the can and poured out the beer. 'Tyson was what they call a drop-out. I don't think he had ever been to prison but he had lived for a long time on the fringe of things. He was about my age and we had a lot in common, so I ended up by sharing a room he had in a tumble-down tenement near the docks.'

Wycliffe could not help looking round at the gleaming plastic and the spotless upholstery.

'He was an educated man and we talked endlessly. We used to go off together on crazy excursions for no reason at all. One evening he told me that he had been born in a little place called Liss which is north of Petersfield and he said, "I'll show it you, we'll go there tomorrow . . ." And we went. Of course we thumbed lifts and it was one of those lifts, on the way back in the evening . . .'

It was obvious that he was deeply disturbed by the recollection and Wycliffe could not help being moved. He reminded Wycliffe of a suffering animal, not because he was unintelligent but because he was deprived of the usual outlets for pain and grief. His features were blank and his words came in the same slow, monotonous sequence like a dripping tap.

'It's difficult to explain. When I recovered consciousness I was

184

in hospital. After a bit they told me that my friend, Morley Tremain, was dead, he had been killed in the crash ... At first I couldn't understand what they were talking about but after a time I worked it out, somehow or other they had got us mixed up. I hadn't the heart nor the energy to explain then and days later, when a policeman called, I gave my name as Tyson, Walter Tyson—just like that. I'd never really thought about it, it just happened.

'It was weeks afterwards that I realized how they had made the mistake. I had an overcoat and a mackintosh but Walter had neither and when the accident happened he was wearing my mack with my wallet in the pocket. In a stupid sort of way I still thought that I would put things right, but everybody was calling me Tyson and the longer it went on the more difficult it was to do anything about it. They asked me if I had any relatives and I told them "No." To cap it all the old van that had picked us up turned out to be unlicensed and uninsured. Everybody was very sympathetic but it meant nothing to me, less than nothing.

'By this time I was moving about the hospital but I still had bandages on; then, one morning, they took the bandages off and I saw myself in the mirror for the first time. You would think I would have been shocked, they thought so and did their best to reassure me. But I wasn't shocked, not a bit. I can remember looking at myself and thinking, "Mother wouldn't know you; you don't recognize yourself." '

Tremain finished the beer in his glass. He was gaining confidence and with it his articulation was improving. Probably he had few occasions for sustained speech.

'I know it sounds odd but from that moment I had a new zest for life. It was as though I had been given a fresh start. Morley Tremain, the man who had served a life sentence for murder, was dead; there was a death certificate to prove it.

'The accident happened in early January and in the last week of March I discharged myself from hospital. It was a beautiful early spring day and it made me feel more than ever that life was beginning again. I went straight to the room I had shared with Tyson and found things just as we had left them. I went through what was there and took everything which would help to identify me with him. I also found a small hoard of money, nearly two hundred and fifty pounds, and I took that too. I suppose he was keeping it as a kind of insurance... I must say it surprised me very much for I have never known a man who seemed more committed to his manner of life but I suppose we all have our final, secret reservations.'

He stopped talking and sat staring at the carpet.

Wycliffe sensed that he had come to the end of a chapter, that he now had to make a great effort to convey something of the psychological and emotional leap which had taken him into his new life and brought him to his present situation. The clock on the wall showed a quarter to one. The wind was still roaring over the site but the rain, no longer continuous, came in driving squalls.

'Why did you come at night?'

'Because I thought we should be undisturbed.'

Tremain nodded. 'That was considerate.'

Wycliffe was reflecting on what he had heard. The boy who had been almost throttled by his mother's apron strings was a man at last.

'Would you like to make a hot drink?'

Tremain brightened. 'Coffee?'

'Suits me.'

Wycliffe would never speak of this night to anyone. They made coffee together in the little kitchen and, automatically, Tremain washed out the milk saucepan and put it away before they carried their mugs back into the living-room.

'The first thing I did was to buy myself some decent clothes and I found a room in a small hotel while I made up my mind what to do next. It was an advertisement in a newspaper which decided things for me, an advertisement for this camping site. "Touring facilities for campers and caravanners. Vans for hire by the week, month or season."

'The temptation was irresistible. I telephoned the number given and booked a van for a fortnight.' He hesitated. 'You must understand that I had no intention of doing anything, I just wanted to see. It was difficult to believe that things were going on there, the same people, the same places... Do you understand?'

'I think so.' It was Wycliffe's intention to let him talk as long as he talked to the purpose, but it was essential to link his story with what other evidence there was. 'You have not mentioned a letter from Ella Jordan.'

Tremain made a vague gesture. 'That came too late, while I was living with mother in Southampton. I burnt it without mentioning it to her. I could not have stood any re-opening of the case. Anyway, I had no idea what importance they would attach to the word of a sick old woman.'

'Go on.'

'No, you don't understand. At that time I had no desire to be—to be vindicated—none whatever. I just wanted to forget.' He added, 'I still do.'

'I accept that.'

Even so the interruption had broken the thread of his narrative and he had difficulty in taking it up again.

'I can't explain to you the effect it had on me to see the village again. It was early in the season and there were not many people about, the site here was almost empty... It was really like going back in time. I can remember the first time I saw Cedric and Eunice...

'At first I was nervous of being recognized but after a day or two I went out of my way to confront people who had known me well, it became a sort of game... I spent a lot of time in the bar.

'The farmer who owns this site was running it himself at that time with help from the casuals and as I had nothing else to do I gave him a hand. I got to like him and I think he liked me. Anyway the long and short of it was he offered me a job for the season and I took it.'

He was aware that his story had become disjointed and he made a new effort to give it coherence.

'At that time I felt no bitterness against anybody. I could meet them and talk to them without hating them. In fact it gave me a feeling of superiority to know what they did not know. I took a great deal of trouble not to make mistakes; it is so easy to speak to someone in a familiar way when, as far as they are concerned, you don't know them from Adam.

'At any rate I worked through that summer and the farmer asked me if I would like a permanent, full-time job as warden. I accepted and he arranged for me to have this van. You must understand that I still had no plan, no wish to *do* anything...'

Wycliffe had his pipe out and was filling it. 'What changed things?'

There was a long silence. Wycliffe lit his pipe and started to smoke in quick, short puffs. The wind was dropping and the rain squalls were less frequent. It was two o'clock.

'I doubt if I can tell you, it is too complicated and I'm not sure that I know myself.' He stretched out his legs and winced as though the movement gave him pain. 'To start with, I left Portsmouth in a mood of frothy optimism and without really coming to terms with what had happened to me. I mean, the accident. I told you that the sight of my own face did not shock me but I soon began to realize that it shocked other people. I came to expect the quick look and the even quicker look in any other direction, or worse, the stare when people thought that I hadn't noticed them. It would take a psychologist to explain why I should hold that against my relatives but I did.

'But there was much more to it than that...' He paused then went on, 'The longer I stayed here the more I realized what a *mess* they had made of their lives. They had got nothing out of it either. My uncle spent his time brooding over his money and plotting against his own children... Cedric was in debt and he had indulged himself to such an extent that he was a physical wreck... Eunice nagged and schemed to get the last penny out of her father and treated her husband like a half-witted servant... They had had the years they took from me and this was how they used them . . .' He broke off. 'Can you understand?'

'I think so.'

'I doubt it. I don't understand myself.' For the first time Wycliffe thought he could detect a note of despair.

'In prison I tried to educate myself, you have to do something or go mad. And when I came here I took up the cudgels again. The idea was to achieve detachment and just when I seemed to be succeeding . . .

'It started by chance. The woman, Ritter, took one of the permanent vans and she was regularly visited by a man she said was her brother. But I knew him. I had spent the last two years of my sentence in an open prison and he was there, though, of course, he didn't recognize me. He is a professional con-man and blackmailer as you probably know. I knew, and I imagine he did too, that his girl was sleeping with Cedric.

'I'm not proud of what I did. I wrote him an anonymous letter which I knew would bait him into blackmailing Cedric and for months I sat back and watched Cedric becoming more and more frantic. It was a form of refined cruelty for which I make no excuse They say the appetite grows by what it feeds upon and this was true in my case. To make Cedric wriggle and squirm was not enough and what had started in contempt ended in hatred. All the pent-up bitterness of the years seemed to flow out of me and to focus on him.

'It was my uncle who gave me the idea when he said, "Sometimes I wonder whether that boy of mine can wait."

'It seemed so logical, so just. I was—I was captivated by the idea and I worked on it as an artist must work on a picture which he knows is going to be *right*.

'I did not expect to kill my uncle, though in my eyes he was as guilty as Cedric. It would have been enough for me if Cedric had been charged with the attempt and had seen the inside of a prison.'

He stopped speaking and it was obvious that, as far as he was concerned, all had been said. He was lying back in his chair and

Wycliffe could see no trace of colour in his distorted features. He was exhausted.

'Where did you learn about explosives?'

'In prison. For four years I shared a cell with a man called Milligan.'

'Gus Milligan?'

Tremain nodded. 'The safe-breaker; the finest peterman in the business. Or that's what they say. He used to boast that he could blow a safe without waking the baby in the next room . . .' A curious sound which must have been a laugh. 'He was good to me and he seemed to take a pleasure in teaching me about locks and safes, about explosives, fuses, and detonators . . . He was a marvellous draughtsman apart from the rest and he used to pass the time by drawing out plans . . .'

Wycliffe stood up to stretch his legs and flex his arms. Tremain would have risen also but Wycliffe signed to him to remain seated. Both men seemed to realize at the same moment how quiet it had become.

'The wind has dropped.'

Both of them glanced at the clock. Half-past two.

Wycliffe remained standing. 'When did you realize that it was Cedric who killed her?'

Tremain did not answer at once. 'I think that it was during the trial when they all lied about him being in bed that afternoon. It dawned on me then that I had actually seen him running away.' He passed his hand over his face.

'So that Ella Jordan's letter was merely confirmation?'

'Yes, and fifteen years too late.'

He lapsed into silence and stared at the carpet. The ticking of the clock seemed to fill the room. 'I've never understood why he did it. He was a violent man but why kill Alice? He had nothing to gain—nothing.' His voice, which had been monotonously steady throughout, had a tremor in it at last.

Wycliffe sat down again. 'I don't think he meant to kill her, he was drunk.'

Tremain seemed to turn this thought over in his mind. 'We

all live on a knife-edge but some of us don't realize it until it's too late.'

Another long silence, broken at last by Wycliffe. 'You have no more explosive or detonators?'

'What? Oh, no—none.'

Wycliffe looked at the disfigured man and his face was expressionless. 'I shall do nothing, do you understand?'

Tremain looked up. It was impossible to tell from his mutilated features what was passing through his mind but he answered, calmly, 'I understand.'

Wycliffe was looking round the room, vaguely, he seemed unsure of himself, perhaps reluctant to leave, to finally commit himself. At last he picked up the buff file and slipped it into his briefcase.

'I must go.'

Tremain saw him to the door as he might have any casual visitor. The night was almost still and the stars were coming out.

'Good night, Mr Tyson.'

Tyson stood at the door of his caravan while the chief superintendent got into his car and drove off; he was still there long after the sound of the car had died away. Then, moving uncertainly, he went inside, closed the door and stood in his kitchen. He felt as though he had just awakened from a long and troubled sleep, as though he needed to repossess himself. He was cold. He felt in his pocket and came out with a small bottle containing a few tablets, he held it in the palm of his hand for a moment, then dropped it into the waste bin. His face, as always, was expressionless but he shook his head in a gesture of firm negation.

Wycliffe had pulled into the deserted car park at the bottom of the hill, left his car and walked. There was a single street lamp burning in the square but otherwise the village was in darkness until he came out on to the waterfront where the navigation lights seemed to burn the brighter. There was still a breeze off the sea and waves still slapped the quay wall. He stood in the shelter of *Green Lady IV* to light his pipe.

He had made his decision. In the morning he would return

Gill's file with a note. No observations. Pilate washing his hands? But Pilate could not absolve himself.

Next morning the sky was clear and a fresh breeze continued to whip up a choppy sea. At breakfast he was aware of Helen's concerned glances but she said nothing of his all but sleepless night.

'I suppose you will be tied up today?'

'No, from now on I'm on holiday. Where shall we go?' He spoke lightly but she was not deceived.

They had scarcely returned to their room when the telephone rang.

'I have a call for you, Chief Superintendent.'

It was Bellings, the deputy chief, as smooth as ever.

'Oh, Charles, I wanted to catch you before you go off for the day. Gill told me that he had sent you the file on his case. I hope you haven't put in too much time on it, you are supposed to be convalescing. In any case it all goes for nothing now, the man is dead.'

'Who is dead?'

'Tremain, of course, the accused. Apparently they've had him in hospital ever since the remand and last night he just died in his sleep. Heart. Not unexpected, I gather. They telephoned me first thing.' Bellings sighed. 'So that's that. Untidy but it saves the taxpayer a good deal of money.'

'What about the man's relatives here?'

'Don't worry, I've been on to division, they'll see to that.' Wycliffe replaced the receiver.

Helen was watching him. 'Something wrong?'

'Wrong? I'm not sure.'